"It was finis... ago."

Aidan's mouth turned down. "Oh, was it, now?" His voice was low. "Then why did you come to my house?" He moved closer, his eyes locking with Gwen's.

Gwen's heart began to beat wildly. He was too damned intimidating. Too male, too overpowering.

"Stay away from me," she said shakily.

He looked at her with hooded grey eyes. "What are you afraid of?"

Ever since **Karen van der Zee** was a child growing up in Holland she wanted to do two things: write books and travel. She's been very lucky. Her American husband's work as a development economist has taken them to many exotic locations. They were married in Kenya, had their first daughter in Ghana and their second in the United States. They spent two fascinating years in Indonesia. Since then they've added a son to the family as well. They now live in Virginia, but not permanently!

Recent titles by the same author:

FIRE AND SPICE

THE OTHER MAN

BY
KAREN VAN DER ZEE

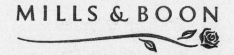

MILLS & BOON

*MILLS & BOON and the Rose Device
are trademarks of the publisher.
Harlequin Mills & Boon Limited,
Eton House, 18-24 Paradise Road, Richmond, Surrey, TW9 1SR*

© Karen van der Zee 1995

ISBN 0 263 79350 8

*Set in Times Roman 11 on 12pt
01-9601-47973 C1*

Made and printed in Great Britain

CHAPTER ONE

THE MAN was looking at her, silvery gray eyes probing her face, meeting her eyes. Gwen's heart stood still. She recognized the eyes, if not the rest of him—the unshaven chin, the longish hair.

Aidan. Her body turned to liquid—she couldn't feel her limbs and muscles anymore. Couldn't breathe, couldn't think. All she felt was a wild, overpowering emotion that made her heart pound and her blood churn through her body. Was it fear? Anxiety? Pain? Oh, God, she thought, don't let me faint into my soup. Not with a restaurant full of people watching.

Desperately, she sucked in a gulp of air and tried to focus on Joe's voice rambling on about the book they'd worked on together.

"Yes," she said, having no idea what she was agreeing to. Her hand clenched rigidly around her soupspoon, she glanced out the window in an effort not to look the other way, at Aidan. The small, rustic restaurant perched on the cliffs overlooking the Pacific and she watched the turbulent waves crashing on the rocky outcrops, spraying up white spume. It was June and the days were long and she'd been looking forward to seeing the sun set, but dark, ominous clouds had gathered in front of the sun and the sky looked bruised and angry. Gwen gave a convulsive shiver. She wanted to go home, to the safety of her house. But they'd only just been served their food and she couldn't ask Joe to drive her back so soon. It was nice of him to take her out. He had meant well. *You need to get out, Gwen,* he had said. *You need some time for yourself.*

It took all her strength not to glance over at Aidan. She focused her eyes on her food. Concentrating hard, she ladled in some of her soup—rich, creamy clam chowder. Her favorite soup, soothing and delicious. She was going to choke on it. She put her spoon down, her hand trembling. She couldn't swallow. She couldn't breathe.

Twelve years since she'd last seen Aidan. What was he doing here now? She glanced back at him—the need was too strong. There was gray in his hair now, hair that was a little too long and unruly. He looked older, more muscular, tougher. All the polish and shine were gone. Even his silver-gray eyes had a tarnished look about them. His face was brown and more angular than she remembered.

He was with a woman, an attractive woman in her thirties with short black hair and large, expressive eyes. She was talking animatedly, using her hands, looking serious.

His wife.

It shouldn't hurt, of course. She shouldn't feel this sharp, jagged jealousy in her chest. She'd known he had a wife for years, but seeing her now made it more real.

My own fault... my own fault...

Aidan turned his head suddenly, as if he'd felt her regard, and again their eyes met. Her heart gave a sickening lurch. She stared, mesmerized, not able to look away from the pale, hypnotic gaze of his eyes.

"Gwen? What's wrong?" Joe's voice was worried.

Tearing her gaze away from Aidan, she pushed her chair back. "Excuse me. I'll be right back."

Her legs were trembling so much it was a miracle she made her way out of the restaurant dining room and into the ladies' room without collapsing between the tables. She suppressed an hysterical little giggle, imagining the scene. Leaning on the cold ceramic of the sink, she closed her eyes. *Calm down*, she ordered herself. *Get a grip on yourself. So he's back. Big deal. Twelve years is a long time. It's all history now. Think of something else—the book, the baby, anything.*

Turning on the tap, she ran cold water over her wrists, splashing water on her silk dress. Periwinkle blue, matching her eyes.

She looked at her face in the mirror. She was ashen and her eyes had a wild, desperate look in them. She closed her eyes and moaned, seeing the man's face in front of her lids. He looked strange with that dark stubble on his chin, but his eyes she would have recognized in a crowd.

Aidan.

Tears flooded her eyes. "Aidan," she whispered, wanting to hear his name. "Aidan."

She didn't want to feel this way, this terrible pain—a pain full of longing and regret. Where had all that come from so suddenly? So intensely? These feelings shouldn't have been there anymore; they should have been long gone, fled with time, buried in forgetting.

She had to get back to the table. She couldn't stay here forever and hide. Swiftly, she pulled a comb through her hair, remembering it had been much longer twelve years ago, remembering Aidan playing with it. *In the sun it looks like polished mahogany*, he'd once told her, which to her had seemed a wonderfully exotic name for brown. Oh, please, she told herself, stop remembering things! Putting on some fresh lipstick, she willed herself to be calm. Smoothing the long, slim skirt of her dress, she walked out of the ladies' room, head high.

Aidan. Looking at her. Oh, God. All her fragile control vanished.

He lounged by the large potted palm, hands in his cotton Dockers, looking tall and imposing in the small entryway. Familiar yet alien. Overpowering. Dangerous.

He didn't even look like the man she remembered. The beard stubble gave his face something faintly sinister. His clothes were new, but were just the standard cotton trousers and striped, short-sleeved shirt available everywhere. The man she remembered had worn expensive, designer clothes, had had immaculate haircuts and a clean shaven chin. And a smile in his eyes. There was no smile now. His eyes were a disturbing gray that shrouded darker emotions.

"Hello, Gwen," he said evenly. "I thought it was you." His voice, deep, masculine and intimately familiar, slid like expensive brandy through her system—smooth and fiery, spreading a treacherous heat.

It took a moment before she could make her tongue move. "Hello, Aidan," she returned, hearing the odd, husky tone in her own voice.

For a timeless moment they stared at each other, the heavy silence ripe with old memories and new emotion.

"How have you been?" he asked at last, his tone cool and polite. Yet deep in his eyes she saw a dark turbulence that contradicted the calmness of his face and voice.

"Fine." She crossed her arms in front of her chest, hugging herself. Cooking smells wafted in from the kitchen—garlic, grilled seafood, something fruity. "I didn't know you were back." Of course she didn't. There was no reason for her to know, no way she could have known. Twelve years had gone by since she'd last seen him and the only information she'd had about him she had found in a newspaper article. As a doctor he'd made an international name for himself in tropical pediatrics, working with children in hospitals in poor, Third World countries. At the time of the article, he and his wife, also a physician, were heading up an impressive medical research project in Asia.

And now he was back in Oregon.

"Just for a few months," he said. "I'm staying at the summer house."

His parents' summer house by the beach, a few miles to the south. Not your average, simple summer cottage, but a luxury beach house high on a cliff with lots of glass affording magnificent views.

She'd stayed there, slept in the big bed with him. Was he sleeping in the same bed now with his wife? *Don't think, don't think*.

"How are your parents?" she asked, putting herself on automatic pilot, trying to be polite, steering away from the personal.

"They're doing well. Just embarked on a cruise around the world." A small pause. He rubbed his chin, something dark and unfathomable in his eyes. "I understand your mother died."

He hadn't liked her mother. She swallowed. "Yes." She'd become seriously ill a month after Aidan had left the country twelve years ago and had died three months later. "It's a long time ago," she added.

Only it didn't seem like it, not now, standing here, seeing him again. All the feelings were still there, all the anguish, as if it had been days instead of years. How could that be, how could that be?

"Yes," he said. His gaze swept over her with cool appraisal, taking in her silk dress, the jewelry, her expensive shoes. "Life appears to have treated you well," he stated. There was no inflection in his voice—his words just a simple, clinical observation, yet the slight, downward tilt of the corners of his mouth gave him away.

"Yes." It was the truth, yet she could well imagine the things he was thinking, seeing her like this, knowing what he knew. She swallowed hard, not knowing what else to say, wanting desperately to get away. She felt young again, and awkward and confused and she hated herself for it. She was almost thirty years old, not eighteen.

"I have to go," she said.

He made a gesture with his hand, indicating the dining room. "Is he your husband?"

So he had known. Somebody had told him she'd married. But obviously his information wasn't up to date.

She shook her head. "No. Marc... my husband died a year and a half ago." Her voice trembled. "I've got to go." She didn't want some polite platitude he'd utter for the occasion. She fled back into the dining room and sat down across from Joe, almost tipping over the wineglass as she reached for it clumsily. From the corner of her eyes she noticed Aidan sitting down again at his own table across from his wife.

"I was about to send out a search party," Joe commented, his brown eyes searching her face. "Are you sure you're all right?"

"I'm fine now," she lied.

"Your soup's cold."

"It doesn't matter. I had most of it. It was delicious. Now tell me more about your ideas for another book." She sat back, determined to give him her full attention, determined not to look again in Aidan's direction.

In August their first book would come out. She had collected the migrant children's stories and drawings, he had taken the photographs. It was a beautiful, poignant collection eliciting smiles, laughter, anger and tears: the stories of forgotten children.

No matter how hard she tried, her mind was not on the book. She was acutely aware of Aidan sitting only feet away, afraid to look up and see his face, see the woman sitting across from him. Afraid to see some small intimacy—a smile, a hand touching the other's. Private gestures that had once belonged to her.

She felt as if she were suffocating. She had to get out of the place, away from Aidan.

She looked up into Joe's face. ''Would you mind terribly if we left? I don't feel right being gone. I need to get back to the baby.''

It was an excuse, and she felt vaguely guilty. Alice, the baby-sitter, was a nurse and the mother of three healthy grown children. The baby couldn't be in safer hands.

She managed to leave the restaurant without looking at Aidan. Outside the wind whipped at her hair and clothes and she dragged in a deep breath of the damp, salty sea air. Joe opened the car door for her and she settled herself in the passenger seat.

For a while the road followed the rugged coastline, offering dramatic views of the wild sea and jagged rocks on the one side, and the wooded mountains on the other. Angry clouds streaked through the sky and violent waves tormented the rocks and beaches. Gwen shivered, feeling a sense of foreboding slithering through her.

Half an hour later she was home, the scent of Poison greeting her as she entered the living room. Alice was sitting on the sofa, feet up, dressed in old jeans and a T-shirt stretched tight across her ample bosom. She was doing a crossword puzzle and the television was off.

The baby was asleep, and had been all the time Gwen had been gone, Alice said, looking distinctly disappointed. "I'd hoped for a bit of cuddling," she added, and gave a long-suffering sigh. Coming to her feet, she gathered her purse and half-finished crossword puzzle. "By the way, do you know a country in Asia that starts with a B? Ten letters."

Gwen's heart made a painful lurch in her chest. "Bangladesh," she said promptly.

"Wow, you're good!" Alice scribbled in the word and frowned. "You didn't even have to think about it."

Gwen shrugged lightly. "Just happen to know."

Alice left, not fazed by the rain, back to her husband of twenty-seven years. The house was silent. Gwen walked aimlessly around, nervous, tense. A big, beautiful, silent house. Marc had designed it for them. He'd been a talented, creative architect who'd designed many beautiful houses for private clients all over the state, Utah and California. Homes built with natural materials that fit the landscape and seemed part of it.

Thunder rattled the windows. She heard the baby cry and ran up the stairs to the room, picking her up out of her crib, holding her close. "It's all right," she whispered. "I'm here, don't cry." She stroked the dark hair, kissed the soft, warm cheeks. The small body squirmed against her, as if fighting a frightening dream. She felt so light, so fragile— much too small for a child of eight months. A lump formed in her throat and she felt overwhelmed by love and tenderness and fear.

She switched on a small light and changed Churi's diaper. She warmed a bottle of milk and sat in the rocking chair, feeding the baby until she fell back to sleep. She sat there for a long time, cradling the warm body against her breast, while tears ran soundlessly down her cheeks.

"I lied, Aidan," she whispered. "I lied."

CHAPTER TWO

"YOU LOOK awful," Alice informed her the next afternoon. "What are you having done? A root canal?" She'd come over to baby-sit Churi while she had her nap so Gwen could go to the dentist. Gwen had planned it that way; she'd be back by the time Churi would be awake again. It made her uneasy to be away when Churi was awake.

"Just a regular cleaning and checkup. I'm fine." Gwen made a casual gesture. "I just didn't sleep well."

Alice grimaced. "That storm was a zinger. The whole house was rattling."

Gwen grabbed her keys and purse and made for the door before Alice would ask more questions. It had not been the storm outside that had kept her awake, rather the storm inside her head that had prevented her from sleeping.

It was a wonderful sunny June day and she opened the roof of the Porsche and drove away. Signs of the storm's destruction were everywhere. The sprawling, neatly manicured gardens around the luxury houses located off the wooded road looked disheveled from the storm's onslaught. Branches and twigs had been ripped off the trees and shrubs and littered the grass. Blooms lay broken and wilted in the flower beds.

Inside Gwen felt as ravished as the gardens. A tight knot of tension in her stomach was growing ever larger. All she'd been able to think about was Aidan, think about that night, twelve years ago, remember the look in his eyes, the sound of his voice, her own.

"Tell me you don't love me!" Aidan's hands hard on her upper arms, eyes wild. "Tell me, dammit!"

Anguish searing through her. "All right! All right! I don't love you!" Tears running down her face. Sobs racking her body. "I don't love you! I don't love you!"

She stared blindly ahead of her at the curving road. "Stop it!" she said to herself. "Just stop it!"

It was not good for the baby for her to be so upset. Churi would feel her distress and there'd been enough distress in her short little life. Gwen bit her lip and clamped her hands hard around the steering wheel. She had to resolve this situation, fast, come to terms with the avalanche of memories and emotions that threatened to take over. She needed to be calm. For her own sake, for Churi's sake. She needed to slow down.

She slowed down, realizing she was on the main road out of town, not even knowing how she'd gotten there. Oh, Lord, her dentist appointment! Too late now. Never mind. She was in no shape to sit in a dentist's chair—quiet, docile, her mouth open, sterile instruments and gloved fingers probing her teeth. She might bite off a finger, or scream. They'd carry her away in a straitjacket. She groaned. A little Valium might not be a bad idea, dentist or no dentist.

It was not a conscious decision to go to the small cove, but an unknown force propelled her there. She parked the car off the road, close to the bushes. The narrow trail was still there, hidden by tangled growth, and muddy from the rains. She clambered down toward the small crescent of deserted beach strewn with debris the waves had tossed up onto the sand the night before. She took off her shoes and dug her toes in the cool sand, wondering why she had come back here now after all these years. Why she was opening herself up to memories that might be better left hidden.

They'd made love on this beach, in the silver light of the moon, with soft breezes cooling their heated bodies. Nights of magic and romance and love.

For a moment she fought the urge to flee, then slowly she lowered herself in the sand and drew up her knees. It was just the way it had been so many years ago: the same sand, the same ocean, the same rocks.

Nothing was the same.

The wind swept her hair back from her face and she closed her eyes, smelling the salty air, hearing the screech of sea gulls. She tried to think of peaceful things. The wind felt good. It came across miles of ocean, from tropical islands with beautiful flowers and palm trees. Hawaii, maybe.

It didn't work. She wasn't in some tropical paradise. She was here, in Oregon, a paradise in its own right with its magnificent wild coast, its majestic, rugged mountains and deep, verdant forests.

And Aidan Carmichael. Aidan Carmichael whom she'd loved so passionately a long time ago.

Aidan in the summer house. Just down the road. She should go see him and get the madness out of her system. Maybe this sort of madness was perfectly normal. After all, he'd been her first true love. He'd been the first man she'd ever made love to and that sort of thing left an impression on a girl's psyche and soul, or so the books said. Usually a bad one, according to statistics.

But it hadn't been bad for her. For her it had been magical.

He'd been caring and loving and gentle. She pressed the heels of her hands against her closed eyes. It was better not to think about this now. It was better to leave it buried like a wonderful treasure—to know it was there, but not to look at it. To leave it hidden in the shadows of the past.

A strand of hair blew across her mouth and she wiped it away. It had been a shock to see him again. Of course it had been, but she could get over it, surely. She was not eighteen any longer. All she had to do was go talk to him and it would be clear that the past was the past and what had been then was over now.

He was a different man now, famous in his field, older, different. And she was different, so different from that frightened, insecure girl she had once been. Talking to him would exorcise the ghosts of the past, the memories, the feelings. He was a stranger now with a life of which she was no part. Once she'd spent a few minutes with him it would become clear that nothing was left of the past and her peace of mind would be restored.

She got to her feet before her courage failed her, clambered up the rocky trail to the place where she had parked her car.

Down the road she went, her heart in her throat, the wind whipping at her hair. Please, please, she prayed. Make all this go away. Make me not feel all these feelings. Please give me back my peace of mind.

She stopped at the narrow path that led to his house hidden in the woods. The weathered wooden mailbox was overgrown with morning glory, the name only barely legible on the side.

She lowered her head on the steering wheel, swamped with trepidation. What if his wife was there? What if... What would she say to him? *I just came to see that I'm really not affected by you anymore. You have changed. I have changed. Life goes on. That's the way it should be.*

I came to say I'm sorry.

Please forgive me.

"Gwen?"

She jerked her head up, heart turning over. Aidan stood by the side of her car, looking down at her. He was bare-chested, wearing only shorts and running shoes, and every inch of his brown exposed skin gleamed with perspiration. His broad chest was lightly covered with dark hair and he was breathing hard. His sleek, muscled body was the picture of male vitality and strength, exuding a rugged, elemental virility. She smelled the scent of pine and tangy sea air and the earthy scent of warm, damp skin.

He wiped his forehead with a blue-and-white striped sweatband wound around his wrist. "Here we meet again," he said, and his deep voice stroked her nerves and tingled through her blood.

Her throat went dry. She swallowed, unable to produce a sound, knowing she was staring at him wide-eyed, looking stupid, her hair wild and wind-blown. She must look like a madwoman. She *felt* like a madwoman.

His eyes swept over her red convertible, his face faintly mocking. "Nice car," he said, his voice carefully bland.

Nice car was an understatement, of course. It was a luxurious, expensive vehicle, a dream come true for many people. Marc had given it to her for her birthday two years ago. She hadn't asked for it. It had never occurred to her to want a luxury sports car. And she'd never wanted the expensive jewelry and beautiful presents Marc was always giving her. "Please," she'd say time and time again, "you don't need to give me all these expensive things. It's not me, Marc. You already give me everything I need." Once, he'd looked at her with eyes full of dark emotion. "Really?" he'd asked, and her heart had constricted at the anguished tone in his voice. Even now the memory made her heart ache.

He had not stopped giving her gifts.

"Have some fun," he had said when he'd presented her with the Porsche. "Live a little."

She remembered the words, but she couldn't remember his face. Panic surged through her. *She couldn't remember his face*! How could she not remember the face of the man to whom she'd been married for more than ten years? All she saw was Aidan—the light eyes in the dark face, the square, stubbled chin, the hard chest. All she was aware of was the disastrous effect he was having on her nervous system and the terrible hunger deep inside her.

"Something wrong?" Aidan asked.

She swallowed again, glancing away at her hands, trembling in her lap, her tongue paralyzed. She shook her head.

"I need something to drink," he went on when she remained silent. "Come on up and join me." Matter of fact. Casual. As if she were a friend, a neighbor. Yet behind the calm words she sensed a subtle command. He was used to having his way, to be obeyed. There was a sense of authority about him that seemed more pronounced than she remembered. It was there in the way he held his body, the enigmatic face, the cool look in his eyes.

She nodded, not sure why. One part of her wanted to run, the other part wanted to do as he suggested. Her hand trembled as she put the car into drive and turned into the path, following Aidan as he jogged up to the house. Powerful legs, broad shoulders. He was a well-constructed running machine, well-proportioned. She watched the smooth movement of his muscles beneath the tanned skin of his back and legs and felt her mouth go dry. Why couldn't she have found him wearing baggy sweats?

She parked the car by the side of the house. Aidan opened the door for her and with a sweeping gesture indicated the back door of the house that led into the kitchen. The front door was never used, she remembered, only when strangers rang the bell.

The big, eat-in kitchen had changed little. It was light and bright with casual but expensive wooden furniture and was updated with the latest appliances. Not your average summer cottage this was, furnished with castoffs and attic furniture. Only the best for the Carmichaels. How awed and impressed she'd been by the family's wealth when she'd been younger. How young and unsophisticated she had been ... Sometimes, looking back, it amazed her how much she had changed, how much she had matured.

The windows had a view of wooded, rugged rocks jutting out into the wide expanse of ocean. She heard the call of sea gulls and the roaring of the waves.

He stood by the sink and splashed water on his face and neck, then dried off with a flowered kitchen towel he pulled out of a drawer.

"You look different," she said, knowing she sounded inane, saying it just to break the awkward silence.

He shrugged as he filled two tall glasses with ice and water. "So do you."

Of course she did. She was twelve years older. And a lifetime wiser. She searched her mind to think of something else to say. "Where were you working, before coming here? Bangladesh, still?"

"No, Ecuador. I left Bangladesh three years ago." He handed her one of the glasses.

He gulped down the entire glass of water, then refilled it. She watched his hands work the tap. Big hands capable of gentle touch. Swiftly, she forced the thought away.

He turned back to her, regarding her with unfathomable eyes. "Why did you come here?" he asked casually, tipping back his glass and drinking more water.

The question she dreaded. "I..." She gestured helplessly, scrambling for words, for a light touch. "I suppose just out of ordinary curiosity." She managed a breezy smile. "To see how you'd fared after all these years."

He cocked one dark eyebrow. "Really?" A single word, a thousand hidden meanings.

She sipped at her water. "Why are you staying here?" she asked. "Vacation?"

He pushed his damp hair away from his forehead. "No. I'm here to finish a book about my research project. Then I'm going back to Ecuador." He placed his empty glass back on the counter.

"Are you ever planning to come back home for good?"

He leaned lazily against the counter, his arms crossed in front of his chest. "Not a great need for tropical pediatrics in the temperate Northwest, is there?" Faint amusement in his voice.

She shrugged lightly. "No. But I suppose you could teach or write, or both."

"I'd rather practice medicine, with a little writing on the side for a change of pace."

They were having a calm, simple conversation, yet she felt shaky with tension. There was so much she wanted to say, so much to explain, but she could not find the words. Her mind seemed to have shut off, as if overloaded with emotion and stress. Then again, why would it matter to him at this point? He had the life he wanted and a wife who shared it, and the past did no longer matter. She wondered where his wife was.

"And what are you doing with yourself these days?" he asked politely.

She moistened her lips. "I'm a teacher. Kindergarten. Five-year-olds."

His eyes narrowed slightly. "Really?"

Had she seen a glimpse of surprise in his eyes? She nodded. "I...I love it. It's vacation now, though, so I'm not working," she went on, feeling ridiculously nervous, as if she were making an uncomfortable confession. "Usually I volunteer in the summer and work with special programs for migrant kids, but...eh, not this time."

Why was she saying all this? Because she wanted his approval, to show him she was not merely a lady of leisure, driving a Porsche and living off her deceased husband's money. She was a person in her own right, a person who had matured and made something of herself.

He studied her. "You look good," he said bluntly. "You lost that scrawny look."

To her mortification, heat rushed to her cheeks. She'd been thin at eighteen, working too many hours, eating too little food. She'd filled out a little in the past twelve years, she knew. She'd gained some weight and rounded out in all the right places.

"I'm not a teenager anymore," she said, as if he didn't know. Why did she have to sound so stupid?

The years of separation yawned between them. How did she bridge that gap of time—all the events and changes that had taken place in the years stretching between then and now? Was it even possible? Did she want to?

"You're a woman now," he agreed, his gaze sliding over her body with seeming clinical assessment. Hidden behind the cool gray something stirred that set off a tingling in her body.

Her heart throbbed in her throat. She swallowed painfully. "I was very young when we knew each other, Aidan." It was more than a statement—it was a plea for his understanding.

"Eighteen." His voice was stone hard. "Old enough to marry Marcos whatshisname." His eyes were gunmetal gray as he stared at her with a sudden cold anger that made her heart turn over.

There was nothing she could say to that, nothing that would make any sense to him. Yet she did not want to be affected by his anger. She had come to peace with her own past and she didn't want to be dragged back into it by his anger. Only she was, whether she wanted to or not. It was as if a storm had tipped her little boat upside down and she was hanging on for dear life, trying not to drown in the turbulent waters.

She wished she were not affected by him so. She didn't want to feel that churning hunger inside her, that pull on her senses just being in his presence.

After all these years, it was still there—the same magnetism, the same power.

What had she hoped for? That her memories were only the feelings of an eighteen-year-old? Romanticized, idealized? That perhaps now that she would see him with the eyes of a mature, grown woman, he would somehow seem diminished, that his strength and male appeal would not seem nearly as devastating to her now as it had been before? She'd been wrong. It was still all there and more. He exuded a raw, wild sensuality that she hadn't known or recognized before and to which she reacted instinctively now. Maybe it had not been there then, or maybe it took a mature woman to sense it.

In the silence she saw his face relax, take on again the look of cool detachment. He waved at a chair. "Sit down."

She sat down. "How did you know I was married?" she asked, clasping her trembling hands in her lap.

He shrugged. "Somebody sent me the announcement that was in the newspaper. I don't remember who." He refilled his glass with water. "I seem to remember his name was Spanish. Mexican?"

"Yes. Marcos Silva. He was born in California, but his parents came from Mexico."

"What did he do for a living?" He tipped his glass back and took a long swallow of water.

She watched his Adam's apple move as he swallowed the water. "He was an architect. He designed private homes for people."

He nodded. "A much better choice than I, I'm sure. Your mother must have approved." A wealth of meaning hid behind those coolly spoken words. Hot indignation flared through her. She forced herself to stay calm.

"She never knew him."

His brows quirked fractionally. "I see."

No, you don't, she almost said. *No, you don't see a thing, Aidan*! She fought the impulse to explain, to make him understand, but she knew it would all sound wrong and he was in no frame of mind to accept her words. Pride kept her silent.

She did not know him this way, those cold eyes, the hard mask of his face. This was not the same man she had once known—not by a long shot. So why then did he still ignite a fire in her blood? Why then did he make her heart race? He was not the open, enthusiastic young doctor she had so loved when she was young. Why then did she still feel the vibrations? Still the yearning? Was it merely a reaction to long-ago memories, rather than the present reality?

She glanced away, out the window, seeing from the corner of her eye that he pushed himself away from the counter. He came toward her, towering over her, and fear assaulted her. He was too close, too potently male, and she felt exposed and vulnerable. He reached for her hands and pulled her to her feet. She was trembling on her legs as she looked into his face, so close, so very close. The heat of his bare chest radiated onto her arms. She felt his breath on her face, smelled the male scent of him—clean sweat, warm, damp skin, salty sea air.

Her body tingled and ached and she couldn't find air to breathe. She wanted to put her mouth to his chest and taste him, lose herself in his nearness. *No*! *No*! She didn't want to feel this terrible hunger, this aching need for something she'd tried for years to forget. Panic assaulted her and she fought against it. *No, no!*

She struggled for air as his eyes locked with hers, felt her heart slam into her ribs and then his mouth was on hers. Firm and hard and sensual. The kiss did nothing to assuage the pain, nor the panic, nothing to melt tension. It started a fire inside her— a fire fed by the still-familiar taste and smell of him, the feel of his hot mouth, his hard body pressed against her.

No! No! She fought ancient instincts, struggled against him, tore her mouth from his. Finally, he released her and stepped back. Gwen leaned against the table, trembling violently, gasping for breath.

"What...the...hell...was...that...for?"   she managed on a furious tone, finding a frightening well of anger. Anger at herself for feeling the way she did now. Anger because he had no right to do this.

Anger because she was terrified. Nothing but heartache and disaster lay ahead if she allowed this to affect her.

He shrugged, a mocking slant to his mouth. "For old times' sake."

"Bastard," she whispered fiercely.

The sounds of a car driving up. A door slamming. She gulped in more air, clasping the edge of the table for support, struggling for composure.

The door swung open and his wife walked in, clutching a bag of groceries to her chest.

"I'm back," she said unnecessarily, and dumped the bag on the counter. She wore a topaz blue shirt and white shorts that showed long, lean legs. She glanced at Gwen. "Hi," she said, and frowned. "Haven't I seen you before? Oh, yes, the restaurant! Last night." She glanced questioningly at Aidan, obviously waiting for an introduction.

"I've got to go." Gwen didn't know where her voice came from. Somehow she made her legs move, forced them to take her out the door and into her car.

Next thing she knew she was out on the road, driving on automatic, going too fast.

He'd had no right to kiss her, to touch her—no right at all. Anger burned inside her. And deep, hot humiliation. He had seen the emotion in her face, sensed the effect he was having on her and he'd taken advantage of it, humiliated her.

"Damn you, Aidan!" she shouted out loud, but the wind whipped away her words.

The sangria was delicious. Alice's daughter, just back from a college semester in Spain, had made it according to a genuine, unadulterated Spanish recipe, which included generous amounts of cognac.

It was getting late, but the party was still going strong and Gwen was having a wonderful time. Her friends had outdone themselves. Flowers everywhere, a pile of birthday presents, wonderful food, a huge, homemade birthday cake.

It was good to have so many friends, to have people care about her and take her seriously. When Marc had died, they'd gathered around her, helping, comforting. And now this. She smiled as she glanced around her garden where they'd all gathered to help her celebrate her thirtieth birthday.

Thirty! It sounded wonderful, as if now she really had grown up and truly was a mature woman. It wasn't what a lot of women thought when they left their twenties, but she didn't mind in the least. She liked it.

It was good to feel independent and secure in yourself and to know what you wanted. It was wonderful to be able to make decisions on your own and to feel confident about your choices and abilities.

She was going to sell this house. She didn't have to ask anyone for permission. She could do it because she wanted to. Because this was no longer her house. It was a place where she had spent a part of her life, a very important part, but that part was over now. Marc was dead and she was no longer a married woman.

She'd sell the Porsche, too, and buy something a little more modest and practical. She grinned to herself. It was wonderful to feel in charge of your own life, to feel so in control.

She had Marc to thank for it all. He had helped her become the person she was now. She closed her eyes for a moment as a wave of guilt washed over her. With an effort she pushed the feeling away and opened her eyes.

Aidan, entering the room from the terrace.

Her heart slammed against her ribs. Oh, God, why was he always showing up when she wasn't expecting him? What was he doing here now? She didn't want him here, in her house. She drew in a long breath of air, fighting for control. *He's not going to ruin the evening for me*, she thought grimly. *I won't allow it*.

He was coming toward her, moving with lazy grace, wearing casual trousers and an open-necked shirt. His chin was smoothly shaven, different than it had been when he had kissed her. She could feel again the roughness against her face, feel again his mouth on hers. Her heart turned over and a sense of humiliation flooded her again. *Get out of my house*! she wanted to call out, but the words stayed frozen in her head as she watched him approach, feeling again the old, familiar pull on her senses, and the frightening sense of having no control over them at all.

Don't let him see how you feel! said a little voice inside her. *Be cool*. She straightened her spine, pulled back her shoulders, gathering strength.

"Happy birthday," he said when he reached her. As if nothing had happened. As if he were a friendly neighbor just dropping by.

She cocked a cool brow. "How did you know?" Her voice was steady. She took a careful sip from her sangria and tried to look relaxed. It took a terrible effort.

He shrugged lightly. "It's the last day of June. I happened to remember, so I thought I'd stop by to congratulate you. After all, thirty years is a milestone. Are you depressed?"

"Heavens, no," she said breezily. "As a matter of fact, I'm delighted."

He surveyed her face for a moment, as if to verify the truth of what she said. "My sister had a nervous breakdown," he said then. "Thought her life was over." A hint of humor, barely perceptible, colored his voice. His eyes did not leave her face.

"Mine's just beginning." She smiled brightly.

His brows rose in question. "How's that?"

"Well, let's say I've finally come into my own. I feel good about myself." She felt a surge of new courage and looked at him squarely. She knew a yearning for him to understand, to know. "I'm standing on my own two feet and I like the feeling." She twirled on her toes as if to demonstrate, her long silky skirt swirling around her ankles. She would not let him spoil her mood. She felt happy surrounded by friends and good cheer.

"Admirable," he said evenly.

"Have a drink," she offered. "We have sangria. The genuine article, straight from Spain. The recipe, that is."

He put his hands in his pockets. "No thanks, too sweet for me."

She gestured at the terrace outside. "The bar is over there, get what you want."

"An impressive spread," he commented, looking at the tableful of food—marinated shrimp, French country pâté, a selection of exotic cheeses.

"I have lots of friends." She smiled brightly. "They did most of it."

Surprise flitted across his features. Gwen knew what he was thinking. Lots of friends. She hadn't had lots of friends when she was younger. She'd been a loner then, shy and insecure, living with her mother in a ramshackle little house at the edge of town. All of that had changed.

He glanced around. "Quite a place," he commented. "You did well for yourself." Just a comment, a simple statement of fact, yet she sensed more than heard the contempt behind the words. Was she imagining it?

There was no reason to feel on the defensive, yet she felt herself tense, she couldn't help it. "Yes, I did," she said flatly, forcing herself to look straight into his eyes. There was nothing there. Nothing but cool, impersonal gray.

The silence throbbed, and suddenly, deep inside that still gray of his eyes she glimpsed something deeper—a dark shadow trying to hide—not anger, not contempt, something else.

He took one of his hands out of his pocket and absently stroked the back of the leather sofa. "I've wondered at times," he said casually, "if you had what you wanted."

Pain. Deep and sharp. She fought not to show him, taking a slow drink from her glass. Her eyes met with his as if drawn together like magnets. Her tongue wouldn't move.

"Did you?" he insisted. "Did you have what you wanted?"

"I was very lucky," she managed, her voice husky. "And I understand you did very well for yourself, too, according to what I've read," she added in a desperate attempt to get away from his line of questioning. "You're doing wonderful work, important work. It's what you always wanted to do, isn't it?"

"Right." His tone was cool, clipped, businesslike.

Something else had changed about him, she realized. There was a stillness about him—in the way he spoke, in the way he moved. Once there had been a restless energy in him, an enthusiasm that caused bright silver sparks in his eyes when he spoke.

From the corner of her eye, she noticed Joe sauntering up to them, his sleek black hair tied back in its usual ponytail. Smiling his warm smile, he draped a protective arm around her. Joe to the rescue, she thought, feeling warm with gratitude and relief. She glanced back at Aidan, seeing his eyes narrowing a fraction.

"Aidan, this is Joe Martinez. Joe, Aidan Carmichael." They shook hands, Aidan's face politely bland, Joe's brown eyes darkly suspicious. He wore his standard garb of jeans and a loose, torrid silk shirt. His cowboy boots were well-worn and well-polished. Next to Aidan in his conservatively casual clothes, he looked rather eccentric.

She slipped out from under Joe's arm. "Excuse me," she murmured, and escaped to her other guests. It was getting late and they were beginning to leave, giving her hugs and smiles and thank-yous which she returned with warmth.

Half an hour later, Joe came up to her. "He's still here. Do you want me to stay?"

She'd been watching Aidan as he'd moved around, exploring the room, not mingling much. He'd studied the Mexican paintings in the living room, stared at the sky outside and he'd perused the books on the shelves.

"He's been looking bored. He'll leave soon." She smiled. "You worry too much about me, Joe." Joe had been Marc's best friend and he was looking after her.

"I don't like the looks of the guy." He frowned. "Who is he?"

She waved her hand casually. "Somebody I knew, a long time ago."

He looked at her searchingly. "I think there's more to it than that."

She bit her lip. "He wanted to marry me, before I met Marc."

"And you didn't want to marry him?"

She hesitated. Her light, frothy mood was deserting her. "I was scared." Just the memory of that primitive, ancient fear made her hands clammy even now, twelve years later. She remembered the nightmares, felt again the dark sense of foreboding she had not been able to shake. *I can't go. Something terrible is going to happen.*

Something terrible had.

Joe frowned at her. "Scared? Were you scared of him?"

"No, no. Please, Joe, I can't go into this now."

He took her hand. "You know, Gwen, I'm here for you. If you need me, let me know, will you?"

She felt a lump in her throat. "I will, Joe. You know I will."

A while later she found herself alone in the silent house. Everyone had gone home and there was no sign of Aidan. He'd left without saying goodnight. She shrugged, feeling relieved that he was gone.

Kicking off her shoes, she sank down on the large Italian sofa and gave a deep, contented sigh. She didn't even have to clean up—it had all been done. All she needed to do was lock up, peek in on Churi, and crawl into bed. She closed her eyes, feeling for the first time how tired she was.

She heard the wind rustle in the trees outside, the cacophony of insects thrilling in the cool night air. Very peaceful. Then she heard footsteps out on the terrace and she froze.

"Gwen?" Aidan's voice.

She bolted upright. "What are you doing here?" Her voice was sharp, out of control.

He shrugged, hands in his pockets. He advanced into the room. "I took a walk—it was a little longer than I intended. Everybody gone?"

She came to her feet. "Yes."

"Your bodyguard, too?" A faint note of amusement. She didn't like it, but she couldn't think of a good retort, so she said nothing and just gave him a cool look.

He glanced down at the small table at the end of the sofa and studied the grouping of photographs arranged on it. She and Marc on a sailing boat, laughing, the wind in their hair. She and Marc sitting on a picnic bench, heads together conspiratorially, his arm around her shoulders. Their wedding picture, both of them smiling. Joe had taken every one of them—beautiful photos, catching just the right expressions, just the right moods.

The air throbbed with tension. Her stomach churned with anxiety as she looked at Aidan's rigid posture.

"You were happy," he stated, a harsh edge to his voice, as if it were an accusation.

She swallowed painfully, her eyes on the photos, fighting a confusion of feelings—a struggle that knotted her stomach and made her chest hurt. The photos blurred in front of her and she clenched her hands into fists. She blinked her eyes, trying to focus on Marc's face, but it was useless. Then she lifted her face to Aidan and met his eyes.

"Yes," she said.

He studied her for a tense moment, taking in the red party dress, his eyes coolly disdainful. "You don't look like a grieving widow to me."

The words hit her like a fist in her chest, then fury flooded her. How dare he? How dare he judge her? She wanted to say something back, something sharp and damaging, but words failed her. The silence echoed with his voice, and the fury mixed itself with guilt, a toxic mixture that lodged itself in her throat, making her wild with a need to lash out.

Then a cry, a frightened cry coming from upstairs. All thought of Aidan, of anger and revenge evaporated. Her body moved instantly, racing up the curving stairs to Churi's room. She lifted the baby out of her crib and hugged her. "It's all right," she whispered. "It's all right, sweetheart. Let's go have some milk."

Holding the whimpering baby against her shoulder, she went down the stairs, stepping more carefully now, afraid to trip over the long skirt of her dress.

Hands in his pockets, Aidan was standing in the middle of the living room, his face expressionless, his eyes the color of old pewter. He said nothing, and there was a curious stillness about him as he gazed at her holding the baby.

She drew in a steadying breath of air. "Get out of my house," she heard herself say. Her voice was not her own. It was hard and frigid and she could not remember ever having spoken that way.

For a moment longer he just stared at the baby, then he turned sharply on his heel and marched out of the French doors into the garden.

How dare he? How dare he? For the next few days, the words echoed in her mind fueling her outrage. Anger was so much easier to deal with than the other emotions—the pain, the longing, the fear. Easier than the ·devastating hunger she felt every time she looked at him. She could not allow herself to feel this way. It was wrong and dangerous.

On Wednesday she took Churi to the doctor for her scheduled checkup. She'd gained a pound. "Excellent," the doctor said, smiling at her. "She's doing great."

Afterward they went to the small town's only supermarket, crowded now with summer tourists who came to the beaches and the mountains. The store was full of the scents of suntan lotion brought in by the people and the fragrance of fresh bread baked on the premises.

With Churi propped up in the baby seat, Gwen pushed the shopping cart through the aisles, picking up bread and vegetables, diapers and baby food, all the while keeping up a conversation with Churi, who looked serious and drooled. A new tooth was coming through.

She met a friend and chatted for a while, discussing babies and baby food brands, then headed for aisle nine to find a can of coffee.

She wasn't the only one looking for coffee, but by the time she realized that one of the three people in the aisle was Aidan, it was too late to turn back; he'd already seen her.

Her heart skipped a beat and started a nervous gallop. Her legs felt oddly weak. Oh, God, she thought, this is so stupid, so stupid. Why does this happen to me? Why can't I just stay calm? She clenched her hands tightly around the cart handle as she forced her gaze to pass over him casually, then return to the shelves.

"Hello, Gwen," he said. So calm, so polite.

She looked back at him. "Hi," she said coolly.

He studied the baby, who gazed back at him with dark, solemn eyes. Gwen glanced at the contents of his cart, seeing a big steak, jumbo shrimp, a bag of rice and assorted other groceries. Perhaps he and his wife took turns doing the shopping.

"How old is she?" he asked, and Gwen's heart slammed against her ribs.

"Almost eight months. Excuse me." She pushed the cart past his and kept on walking.

You should have told him. You should have explained.

I don't owe him any explanations.

As she turned out of the aisle, Aidan's wife turned in, a plastic bag of green grapes in her hand. Gwen kept on moving, pretending she hadn't noticed her, her legs wooden, her chest aching.

At home, she made herself a cup of coffee and a sandwich and fed Churi her lunch. After a nice long cuddle, she tucked her in bed for her afternoon nap.

She had to try not to think about Aidan. She had work to do. She wanted to sell the house. Which meant she'd have to find another place to buy. What place? Where? A little closer to the beach, but not too far from school. Something simple and comfortable and not too big. She'd have to do some looking around, check with a real estate agent. Which one? Joe would know.

"You want what?" he said after she told him of her intentions.

"A real estate agent, to help me sell the house," she repeated. "It's too big, too fancy for me, Joe."

Joe was silent. Joe had been Marc's best friend and she knew what was going through his head. Marc had designed that house for them. They'd lived there almost all their married life.

"I have to move on, Joe," she said quietly.

"Yes, yes, of course." He was all business suddenly, giving her the name and phone number of an agent he knew personally.

"Have you thought about my idea for the next book?" he asked then.

She hadn't thought about anything but Aidan and the baby in the last few days. "I'm sorry, I haven't," she admitted. "Maybe we should see first how well this one sells. It's only a couple of weeks before it's out."

"Yes, of course. I was just thinking of the possibilities."

After they'd hung up she glanced around the house. She'd have to sell or give away a lot of the furniture when she moved to a smaller place.

A place of my own. All my own. Guilt swamped her suddenly, settling like wet cement in her heart. Marc had given her a home, love, security, stability. All the things the scared little girl inside her had needed and craved. All the things her mother had said to look for. No, that was not true.

Her mother had not believed in love.

Love was an overrated, dangerous emotion that existed only in people's fantasies. Love invariably caused grief and disillusionment. Love did not keep food on the table or a roof over your head.

Her mother had been a very disillusioned person.

That night she dreamed of her mother. She looked very old and gray, lying in a white hospital bed, her skin sallow. Her mother was crying. Her mother never cried.

"And what about me?" she was saying over and over again. "What about me?"

"I'm not leaving, Mom. I'm here." Gwen searched for her mother's hand. It wasn't there. She broke out in a cold sweat, searching everywhere under the covers. She couldn't find it anywhere. "I'm not leaving, Mom. Give me your hand. Please, Mom, give me your hand."

"If you go to Africa, I'll be all alone," her mother whimpered.

"I'm not going to Africa, Mom! I'm going to stay with you. Just give me your hand. Please, just give me your hand."

Churi was in her playpen on the terrace while Gwen watered her plants in the wide windowsill of the living room window. The room smelled deliciously of roses. She'd just picked a large bouquet of them in the garden where bushes flourished with abandon. Inside her plants did well, too. Plants were so easy. Just a little care and they grew and bloomed luxuriantly. She liked to take care of things, to see things grow. Plants. People. Babies.

A gleaming, blue-grey Mercedes-Benz came down the road and slowed down, then turned into the driveway. Every muscle in her body tensed and her breath caught in her throat as she noticed Aidan's big frame emerging from the vehicle. He wore faded jeans and a black T-shirt and his hair looked disheveled. His appearance was in odd contrast to the luxury car, which was probably on loan from his globe-trotting parents. It struck her how easy it was to visualize this tough, rugged man in a Jeep or Land Rover. He strode purposefully up to the door.

Why was he here? What did he want?

The doorbell chimed its cheerful tune.

I don't want to see him anymore, she thought desperately. *I want him to stay away from me*. He was shaking up her world, her hard-earned control of her life, her confidence and her peace of mind.

She could not allow him to do that. She drew in a ragged breath. Her chest ached.

She went to the entryway and opened the door.

"Good morning," he said, raking a hand through his hair, as if he realized it needed some attention. It did. He looked in serious need of a shower and a shave.

"Good morning," she returned, forcing her voice to be calm and polite.

It did not appear to be a very good morning for him; he looked exhausted, his eyes weary, as if he'd been up all night. Maybe he'd had a fight with his wife and she'd kicked him out of the house. Maybe he'd slept in his car. It did not seem a likely explanation. Aidan Carmichael was not a man who'd let himself be kicked out of the house.

"What are you doing here?" she asked, her body tense, forcing herself to look him squarely in the face.

"I want to talk to you." A command more than a statement, and it didn't escape her notice.

She crossed her arms in front of her chest. "Why? Do you want to insult me some more?"

"Insult?" He frowned as if trying to remember what she was referring to, then shrugged lightly. "I was merely stating a fact. In that sexy red dress you looked quite the happy birthday girl."

Well, she had been. She gritted her teeth. "I *was* the happy birthday girl, with absolutely no apologies to make! And I have no intention of standing here arguing with you. You shouldn't be here."

"Oh, yes, I should." Without further ado, he put his hands on her shoulders, moved her aside and stepped into the large hallway. She watched in stunned disbelief as he strode into the living room as if he had every right in the world to be there.

CHAPTER THREE

HIS RUDENESS rendered her speechless for a moment. This was not the Aidan she remembered—the one with the impeccable upbringing and superb manners and sophisticated ways.

Hands clenched, she followed him, furious for his intrusion. "What do you want?" she asked coldly.

He stepped through the open French doors onto the stone terrace, where Churi sat in her playpen playing with her toys.

He put his hands on his hips. "Why don't you introduce us?" he asked, ignoring her question.

"Her name is Churi. I want you to leave."

He smiled at the baby. "Hello, Churi," he said gently.

The baby looked up at him with large brown eyes—eyes that looked too big for her small face.

Aidan glanced back at Gwen. "I'd appreciate a cup of coffee. Strong, please." Another order. Who did he think he was?

Gritting her teeth, Gwen glared at him, her body rigid. "This is not a restaurant."

"I'm aware of that," he said with infuriating calmness. He was looking at the baby again. "Has she been ill?"

"No, she hasn't," Gwen said tightly, feeling her nerves begin to jump. She wanted him gone—fast,

45

now. "You shouldn't be here. This is a small town. People talk."

He cocked a faintly contemptuous brow. "It does not interest me in the least what people might say." He allowed a significant pause. "I do not arrange my life according to the wishes and opinions of others."

As opposed to what she had done years ago— according to his opinion. A wave of hot anger washed over her. She wanted to slap his arrogant face, but with an effort she managed to control herself. For a fleeting instant she heard again his voice, saw his face as he had looked at her that fateful evening years ago. *You can't allow your mother to decide for you what to do, and how to live. You're not thirteen. You've got to live your own life.* She pushed the memory away, curling her toes as if it were a physical effort.

"What do you want?" she asked coldly, wanting not to feel disturbing feelings, trying to block them out.

"There's something we need to discuss."

"There's nothing to discuss."

"Oh," he said lazily, "we can think of something. There's plenty of unfinished business."

"It was finished twelve years ago."

His mouth turned down at the corners. "Oh, was it now?" His voice was low. "Then why did you come to my house?" He moved a little closer, his eyes locking hers.

Her heart began to beat wildly. He was too damned intimidating with those pale, piercing eyes in that dark face. Too male, too overpowering.

"Stay away from me," she said shakily. She felt like a little girl again and she hated it. She hated to feel the insecurity he seemed to evoke in her.

"What are you afraid of?" His voice held faint mockery and she realized he had read her emotions on her face. Desperately, she took a step backward, then another. He didn't follow, didn't touch her, just looked at her with hooded gray eyes she couldn't read.

"How about that coffee?" he asked. "I need the caffeine." He rubbed his forehead and again she noticed how tired he looked.

"And then what?"

He shrugged. "We'll talk."

"What do you want from me, Aidan? An apology? Will that make you leave?"

"No." He swayed on his feet. "I want coffee." His voice was low and grim. "Then we'll talk."

It was obvious that he had no intention of leaving and she could hardly push him out the door. All right, she'd make coffee. She could use a little fortification herself. But he couldn't make her talk. She had at least some control left.

In the kitchen she braced her arms on the counter and let out a long sigh, willing herself to calm her churning emotions. Then she filled the decanter with water, took out a filter and fumbled with the coffee grounds, spilling them all over the counter. She cursed under her breath and swept them into the sink with a trembling hand. Her next attempt at scooping coffee into the basket was more successful. She switched on the coffee maker and took out cups, milk and sugar. The coffee would take a

while to brew. Taking in another fortifying breath,
she made her way back to the living room.

Aidan was sitting in a chair on the terrace with
Churi on his lap.

Gwen froze as she watched the scene in front of
her eyes. She heard his voice, soft and comforting,
saw his hands gently moving over the small body,
checking, examining. Graceful, careful hands.

She felt hot and cold in turns and she stormed
out the French doors.

"What the hell do you think you're doing? Give
her to me!"

He made no move to do so. Churi stiffened at
the angry sound of her voice and gave a cry of fear.

Aidan glanced at Gwen, his face cold. "She needs
medical attention," he said, his voice cool and
clipped.

"She's getting it! Who the hell do you think you
are to come barging in here and examine her?"

That's why he's here! she realized suddenly.
*That's why he wanted coffee, to get me out of the
way*.

Churi was crying now and Gwen reached out to
her. Aidan handed her over without further ado.
Gwen held her close, trying to soothe her. No doubt
the angry tone in her voice had frightened her.

Aidan rose to his feet, towering over her like an
avenging god. "Your baby is malnourished and
underweight! How the hell did that happen?" There
was nothing of the clinical physician in him, no
cool, objective tone in his voice. He was angry,
wildly angry.

Gwen was shaking. "You're the expert, Doctor. You must have seen thousands of malnourished children. How does that usually happen?"

He stared at her, his face hard, and the silence throbbed between them.

She knew the answers. Poverty and ignorance of the parents was one. The other was worse. She soothed the baby, all the while looking straight into Aidan's face, daring him to accuse her, daring him to say one negative word.

A bee buzzed around nearby. The air was heavy with the sweet perfume of roses. Slowly, she saw the anger seep out of him, saw the rigid line of his jaw relax. He raked a hand through his hair, letting out a sigh. His face looked drained.

"She isn't your baby, is she?" he asked on a low note.

"No." She stroked the baby's soft hair, feeling a stab of pain. *I wish she were*, came the unbidden thought, a dangerous thought, a thought that could bring nothing but disappointment.

"Why are you taking care of her?" he asked, eyes slightly narrowed, face intent.

Her throat felt raw. "I want you to leave my house. You have no right to be here and this is none of your business."

His jaw hardened again. "The welfare of children is everybody's business. I'm not leaving until I know what's going on with this child." His tone was hard and uncompromising.

Common sense battled her anger. His interest was no surprise, and certainly nothing to condemn. He was a doctor, a children's doctor, and he wanted to satisfy himself that this child was getting the proper care. She could not fault him for his motivations, but his attitude infuriated her. He'd marched into her house as if he owned the place. He'd suspected her of wrongdoing.

He was a doctor who spent his life in poor countries taking care of helpless children because that was what he wanted to do, felt compelled to do. He hadn't wanted a prestigious, lucrative practice in a big city, although that was what his wealthy, successful parents had expected of him. He'd wanted to take care of the children who needed him most. Eleven years ago she'd been so in love with him, so awed by his dreams and idealism. Aidan was a hero in her eyes. Aidan cared.

Aidan still cared.

Admiration was stronger than anger. She swallowed, feeling a softening inside her. "Social services placed her with me last month. Her parents were in an accident. They'd just got here from Mexico. They're still in the hospital, in pretty bad shape, but they're expected to recover eventually."

"And why did they give her to you?"

"I've been licensed as a foster parent." She stroked the baby's back. "I take her to the doctor regularly. I've been told what and how to feed her and she's gaining weight. She's doing well."

He pushed his hands into his pockets and observed her for a moment. The silence was heavy with unspoken thoughts and questions. She prayed he would leave it that way, prayed he wouldn't ask.

"No children of your own?" he asked quietly.

"No."

"You wanted lots of children," he went on, his tone low and rich with meaning. "I'd expected you to have a number of them by now."

"Well, I don't," she said flatly.

"I'm sorry." He searched her face, waiting.

She bit her lip and averted her eyes, glancing down at the baby's head and gently stroking her back. She was not going to confide in him, tell him how disappointed she had been. The doctors had found no reason for her not to conceive, and it was suggested Marc should see a doctor. He never had.

She didn't want Aidan's pity, or anyone else's for that matter. She also didn't want to continue the conversation. "I'll pour the coffee," she said, trying to sound businesslike. Bending down, she lowered Churi into her playpen.

Alone in the kitchen she found her eyes filling with tears. *You wanted lots of children*, he'd said. It was true. They'd talked about it and he'd remembered, of course he had. Growing up as a lonely only child she'd dreamed of having lots of sisters and brothers, promising herself that later she'd create her own family, have a houseful of children of her own.

It hadn't happened.

She picked up the coffeepot and filled the cups, blinking away her tears.

Did Aidan and his wife have children? There hadn't been any at the house, she was sure. It didn't mean anything. They might be staying with relatives or friends, or in summer camp learning to swim or canoe. Healthy, wholesome children with bright eyes and quick smiles. Two, maybe three . . .

She didn't want to know. Oh, God, she didn't want to know anything about him. It was too painful, no matter what her rational mind told her. She wished he'd never come back.

Footsteps behind her. "Let me give you a hand," said Aidan. He reached for the mugs, then gave a muffled curse as he looked at her.

His face was a blur and she turned away hastily, taking a tissue from the box on the breakfast table and wiping her eyes. Oh, damn, why had he come now? The last thing she wanted was for him to see her weeping.

There was nothing to cry about, really. She was doing just fine. She had friends who loved her, a nice house, no money worries, a wonderful job, and Churi to love and take care of—for a little while. She had so much more than many people, a better life than her mother had ever had. She should be grateful. She *was* grateful. Good Lord, she said to herself impatiently, stop being a sap and feeling sorry for yourself.

She felt Aidan's hands on her shoulders as he turned her toward him. "I'm sorry," he said quietly. "I didn't mean to make you cry. I apologize for suspecting you of...not taking care of your baby." The words came out with difficulty. "It was uncalled for. I, of all people, should have known better." He slipped his arms around her back and held her close.

For a fraction of a moment she felt the comfort, felt he warmth of his body against her own, smelled the familiar scent of him. For a fraction of a moment she remembered all those other times he'd held her in his arms, felt the heat of desire rush through her like wildfire.

His mouth was on hers and passion met passion.

Temptation, such aching temptation.

Then a hundred alarms went off in her head. She pushed against the solid wall of his chest with the strength of panic. "Don't!" she cried. "Don't do this!"

He released her, tension in his face, shadows in his eyes.

"What a rotten thing to do!" she said breathlessly, stepping back from him. Tears slid down her face again and she wiped at them furiously. "What are you trying to prove?"

His face turned expressionless, his eyes empty. "Nothing," he said, his voice oddly toneless.

The phone rang. She turned her back to him and lifted the receiver. Her hand shook. "Hello?" Her voice sounded odd.

It was Marc's mother calling from California. Gwen loved her mother-in-law, but wished desperately she'd have called at another time. She could see the terrace from the kitchen window and Churi was playing contentedly. She spoke in Spanish, as always, with her in-laws. One of the things that had endeared her to them had been her willingness to do so, even though in the beginning her basic school Spanish had not been very good. She'd learned, and several trips to Mexico to visit other relatives of Marc's had helped to make her very competent.

When she hung up the phone five minutes later, she turned and found Aidan gone. Entering the living room, she discovered him sprawled out on the large sofa, dead to the world.

She went around the house doing some cleaning, pretending—trying to pretend—that Aidan wasn't in her living room, asleep. He looked so exhausted that she didn't have the heart to wake him up and tell him to leave. Asleep he couldn't bother her.

At least as long as she didn't look at him, didn't think of the past and all the memories it held.

The windows were open to let in the fresh air and the breeze was fragrant with summer. Such a bright, light, spacious house. Such lovely views of the flower garden and the woods beyond. Yet more and more it seemed she did not belong here anymore, as if deep inside her something beckoned—another dream, another world.

She played with Churi, made a few phone calls, gave Churi her lunch and put her down for her afternoon nap. Aidan was still asleep and looked like he wasn't about to wake up. Standing by the sofa, all her muscles tense, she looked down on his prone body. One brown arm was raised over his head, the other lay on his flat stomach, his fingers curled in a loose fist. Small white lines fanned out from the corners of his eyes. His full mouth was not quite closed, showing a glimpse of white teeth. She watched the rhythmic rise and fall of his chest, wishing she could put her cheek down and hear the strong beat of his heart, as she had done so many times in the past. Uneasiness settled over her. She knew she shouldn't allow herself to think these thoughts, should not be standing there looking at him, wishing she could touch him, wishing she could run her fingers through his hair.

Too late, too late. He was another woman's husband now. Her heart contracted painfully.

Once, many summers ago when she'd been young and poor and full of dreams, this man had been hers. He had loved her. She had loved him.

It had been a magical summer, the summer she was nineteen. She was in love with Dr Aidan Carmichael and he loved her back. He said she was special. Nobody had ever said she was special. Nobody had ever made her feel beautiful and happy to be alive.

Aidan Carmichael was the most wonderful man she'd ever met. She'd worked as a youth counselor at a special summer camp for migrant children and one day a little boy had became ill and she'd taken him to the emergency room at the local hospital. And there was Aidan, dark, tall, wearing a white coat and looking devastatingly handsome. Her heart had stopped when he'd looked at her with his mesmerizing silver-gray eyes and she'd barely been able to answer his questions about the boy's condition and symptoms.

She'd suddenly felt awkward and inept, not at all the confident, competent counselor she was at the camp. Her shorts and shirt were dirty, her bare, sandaled feet dusty, her hair still damp from swimming. Somewhere she probably had some bug or other crawling all over her.

The boy was admitted to the hospital for overnight observation. She stayed with him until his parents arrived two hours later. By then her day shift at the camp was over and she could go home straight from the hospital. As she walked back to her car, Aidan had come out, white coat gone. Her heart had made an odd little leap in her chest. She didn't know anything about men's clothing, but it didn't take an experienced eye to see that his were very classy and expensive.

"You're still here?" he asked.

"I waited for his parents to come."

He smiled at her. "You were very good with him."

"So were you," she said, grinning back. "But then, you have to be."

"So do you, being a camp counselor. Do you speak Spanish?"

"A little. I had a few years in high school, and now I'm learning from the kids. They come from all over, you know—Mexico, Guatemala, Honduras. They're at the camp most of the summer while their parents work." She frowned. "I feel sorry for them."

"Why?"

"It's a hard life for them. Many of them move around all the time while their parents harvest the crops, one after another. Some of them live in cars or campers. They're kids and they've got nothing to say about how they live." She shrugged self-consciously. "Anyway, I'm sure you know all that."

"I've heard about it, and read about it. That's not the same as knowing."

The gentle tone of his voice stirred something deep inside her. "We can never really know, can we?" she asked softly.

He shook his head. "No."

They stood still, looking at each other. She fumbled nervously with her car key, feeling a strange lightness.

"Going home?" he asked.

She nodded.

"You have time for a cup of coffee? Or a Coke?" He waved at McDonald's golden arches across the street.

It was a simple question, but one that came as a total surprise. Men like Dr Carmichael didn't invite her for a cup of coffee. Men like Dr Carmichael didn't usually even *see* her, much less talk to her or ask her to have a cup of coffee.

"I . . . eh, yes, I suppose," she said awkwardly, and felt herself blushing. "I've got to be at work at seven, though."

His brows arched. "Isn't working all day at a summer camp for kids enough of a job?"

They stood at the curb waiting for the light to turn green. "This is my second job, four nights a week. At the video store. It's only three hours, until ten," she added hastily. "I'm saving up for college." The light turned green. She walked along with him, trying to take big steps to keep up with his long strides.

"You won't have time to eat, then," he stated as he held the door open for her.

"I don't usually eat much. It's all right."

Of course he didn't think it was all right, and he insisted on buying her a hamburger along with her Coke in spite of her protestations. They sat across from each other and talked.

Between bites, she told him about her work at the camp and how much she loved playing with children. She told him she wanted to be a kindergarten teacher, that she was an only child and had always wanted brothers and sisters and that later, when she was married, she intended on having a big family. She told him she did not know where her father was and that he had left her mother before she was even born, and that her mother worked as a waitress at a truck-stop restaurant.

After a while she stopped talking, realizing suddenly that she was telling him personal things he couldn't possibly be interested in. Embarrassment flooding her, she came clumsily to her feet. "I've got to go."

What in heaven's name had possessed her to chatter on about herself like that? She sat in her car and drove home on automatic. She wasn't the talkative type; she didn't divulge things about herself to strangers, or even to people she knew. It was mortifying. She had bored him to tears. It was pathetic.

Several days later she found him waiting at the camp's exit as she was leaving for home.

"I thought you might be ready for another hamburger and Coke," he said, giving her a devastating smile.

She couldn't help but grin at him as a rush of joy suffused her. "You're alive," she blurted out, and his brows rose in surprise.

"At least, I think so," he returned, amusement in his voice. "Is that a surprise?"

She felt oddly warm. "I thought you might have died from boredom. I talked too much last week and when I caught myself I was so embarrassed."

"No need to be. I came back for more."

His eyes were laughing and her heart made a dangerous flip-flop in her chest. Birds were singing and the air was fragrant with the sweet scent of newly mowed grass.

It was the beginning of a fairy tale. A fairy tale full of magic and wonder and delicious adventures.

A fairy tale with an unhappy ending.

It was hard to believe that the man asleep on her sofa with the old jeans, the long hair and the unshaven face was the same man as the well-dressed, clean-cut young doctor with his smiling eyes.

Why then did she still feel the same pull? The same terrible yearning?

I can't let this happen, she thought. *I can't feel this way. It isn't right. I've got to stop this madness.*

Dragging her gaze away from him, she turned abruptly, banged her thigh into the side of the coffee table so hard it sent a large photo book skidding across the polished surface to the edge from where it plunged to the floor with a loud thud.

Rubbing her thigh and muttering a curse, Gwen bent over to pick up the book. Aidan opened his eyes, looking disoriented.

"What's going on? Did I fall asleep?"

"You've been dead to the world for hours," she said, putting the book back on the table.

"Good God," he muttered.

"I suppose you were up all night."

He struggled into a sitting position and raked both hands through his hair. "Yes."

She wondered what his wife would think of this state of affairs, if she were worried. "Maybe you should call home," she suggested.

He made a dismissive gesture. "Nobody there." He sighed again. "I know I'm risking your wrath, but could you spare me another cup of coffee?"

She had pity on him. She nodded and went to the kitchen. Had his wife run out on him? Was that why he looked as if he'd been up all night? She groaned as she took out two coffee mugs. "I don't want any part of this," she muttered to herself. "Aidan and his domestic affairs are none of my business." Quickly she made two ham-and-cheese sandwiches and poured the coffee, trying hard not to listen to a small voice inside her telling her she was an idiot to be doing this, that instead she should demand that he leave her house now, this instant. That he should go home and make coffee and sandwiches himself.

She came back into the living room to find Aidan looking through an advance copy of the photo book she and Joe had done together and her heart made a nervous little leap. She put the tray on the coffee table and he glanced up at her.

"Very interesting," he said quietly. "Joe is quite a photographer."

She nodded. "Yes."

"And you collected the stories and the drawings?"

"Yes. Most of them from migrant kids at summer camps. I kept thinking I had to do something with them—find some way for people to read them and know what goes on in their little heads, and what the realities are of their lives." She sat down, aware of his intense gray eyes studying her face.

"I remember the day we met," he said then, "when you came to the hospital with that little boy." He glanced back down at the book. "It's a beautiful book."

"Thank you." She pushed the plate toward him. "Have a sandwich," she offered, not wanting to talk about the past, about the time when everything had been so different between them, when there had been love and hope and dreams. "I was having one for lunch and I thought you might want one, too."

He glanced at the food, then at her face, his eyes meeting hers. "Still the caretaker, are you?" he commented. There was a hidden meaning there, but no hint of condemnation or mockery.

She shrugged lightly. "I figured you hadn't had breakfast."

He took a long drink from his coffee. "True."

"What were you doing all night?" It wasn't any of her business, but the question was out before she could stop herself. "Singing, dancing and drinking?" she suggested lightly, knowing full well that whatever it was, it wasn't that. She bit into her sandwich.

"I lead a secret nocturnal life," he said darkly, "full of evil and debauchery." He grimaced and rubbed his neck. "I was working. We had to get one part of the book finished. Ella had to go back to Berkeley this morning to teach a course and she won't be able to get back here until the end of next month."

Ella. Gwen couldn't swallow. She hadn't known his wife's name, hadn't remembered it after reading the newspaper article. Blocked it out, maybe. Perfect psychological self-defense.

A hundred questions whirled in her mind. She wanted answers. No, she did not. The less she knew the better it was for her peace of mind, the less it would hurt. She got to her feet. "I'll get you some more coffee, and then I think you should leave." She tried to sound calm and businesslike.

"Of course," he said, with the voice of the old Aidan, the sophisticated man who knew his manners—not the one who barged into people's houses, ordered them around and fell asleep on their couches.

His sandwich and coffee finished, he came promptly to his feet. "I apologize for falling asleep on your sofa," he said as they made their way to the entryway. "Thank you for the coffee and the food."

"You're welcome," she said.

He stopped and stared at her with his light eyes and her heart began a nervous dance. She reached for the door and opened it with businesslike finality, willing her heart to slow down.

"Don't worry about Churi," she said, remembering she'd been the reason for his visit.

He shook his head. "No." Then he marched abruptly out the door and toward his car parked in the drive. Gwen closed the door before she saw him get in. Letting out a deep sigh, she leaned her back against the wall and closed her eyes.

"I don't want to see him again," she said out loud. She wanted her peace of mind back, and her confidence. She wanted to forget him. She wanted . . .

She covered her face with her hands and moaned.

Fate was not kind. She found the wallet that evening as it lay snuggled between two sofa cushions. Aidan's. It had to be.

She picked it up, temptation rampant. A wallet was a treasure house of information. Names, numbers, credit cards, photos. Photos of loved ones. A wife. Children.

Just think! a little voice inside her admonished. *Think of what you could find out about him*!

I am not going to go through his wallet, answered another part of her.

Maybe it isn't even his. You should look for some identification, at least. A driver's license should do.

I don't need to. It's his wallet.

She smelled the faint scent of leather. The wallet was brand new, smooth to the touch and a little stiff. Aidan had probably bought it after his return to the country. Fighting the raging temptation, she went to the phone and put the wallet down while she searched the phone directory for Aidan's number.

Even calling him made her heart do jumping jacks. She punched in the numbers with more force than necessary and glanced unseeingly out the window waiting for him to pick up.

"Carmichael," came his voice a moment later, sounding terse. It occurred to her that he was probably working and she had disturbed his concentration. Well, it couldn't be helped.

"It's Gwen. Are you missing your wallet?"

A moment of silence. "Yes. Damn! Did I leave it at your house?"

"I found it on the sofa. I figured it had to be yours."

He sighed. "Well, I'd better come and pick it up now, if that's convenient for you."

"That's fine. I'm home."

Half an hour later Gwen saw the Mercedes come up the drive. She opened the front door, the wallet ready in her hand. She did not intend to invite him in; there was no need for it.

He had changed his clothes, wearing khaki shorts and a green T-shirt. His energetic stride indicated he had overcome his fatigue. He looked full of vigor, his body radiated male appeal. She swallowed and steeled herself against the onslaught of feelings.

She handed him the wallet. "I found it hiding between the sofa cushions. It must have fallen out of your pocket," she commented.

He nodded, taking the wallet from her and sliding it in his back pocket. "Thanks. I'm glad you found it."

"If it had slid down farther, I might not have seen it so soon."

His mouth curved slightly. "Would have been a very unfortunate situation for me." His eyes held hers. "How about dinner tomorrow night?"

She couldn't believe her ears. His wife had barely left the house and here he was asking her out. Anger welled up inside her.

"No," she said tightly.

"Another night?"

Her body tensed some more. "No, Aidan. Not any night. I want you to stay away from me."

One brow quirked up. "I don't believe you." His voice was calm and confident.

She gritted her teeth. "What you believe or do not believe is not my problem."

His eyes narrowed. "Then what *is* your problem? Joe?" He pushed his hands into his pockets. "No offense intended, Gwen, but I can't see you with an artistic, eccentric type with long hair."

She glared at him. "My private life is none of your business. Just know that I don't want you in it."

Something flashed in his eyes, then disappeared. "Not even for an innocent little dinner?" His voice was cucumber cool. "I thought it might be interesting to spend some time together. I find it quite intriguing to see you changed into so mature and sophisticated a woman."

"Save the flattery," she said succinctly.

"No flattery intended." His mouth curved. "What's wrong with a pleasant little dinner and some pleasant conversation?"

"Everything," she snapped. "Everything is wrong with it."

He leaned one hand casually against the door post and observed her with unconcealed curiosity. "Because of Joe?"

"No, because of Ella! I don't go out with married men!"

Surprise flitted across his features. "Ella?" Amazement filled his voice. "Ella's not my wife. For heaven's sake, what gave you that idea?"

His reaction caused instant confusion. "I...eh...it seemed rather obvious," she managed.

"Ella's a colleague. She's a doctor. She worked with me in Ecuador for a while and she's doing part of the book with me." He frowned and rubbed his chin. "I never did introduce you, did I?"

"No." She felt a disorienting dizziness, an odd sense of unreality, as if she'd been turned upside down and the world looked suddenly very different.

Ella was not his wife. Then where was his wife? The one the article had mentioned, the one who'd been in Asia with him? She took in a deep breath.

"What about your wife, then?" she heard herself ask. "The...the one who worked with you in Asia?"

CHAPTER FOUR

AIDAN'S frown cleared. "Sophie, you mean Sophie," he stated. "How did you know about her?"

"I read it in the paper, in an article about you when you were in Asia, Bangladesh." She didn't understand a thing. If he was married to a Sophie, then where was she now? Had she stayed behind in Ecuador, or was she somewhere else visiting friends or family? Were they divorced? Had she died?

She wished there were a chair to sit on, but she was standing in the entryway because she hadn't wanted to ask him in.

He nodded. "I remember that article. Sophie and I weren't married, though. We arrived together and people assumed we were married. Considering the circumstances and the local mores it seemed prudent to just let it appear that way."

"Oh." His words threw everything inside her into even greater turmoil—her image of him and his wife, her feelings toward him and his behavior. Right and wrong suddenly were not what they had been. Her anger at his kissing her had lost its reason. "You're not married, then?" she asked, to make it as clear as it could be, to fix the reality of it into her mind.

"No, and I never have been, and Sophie's been out of the picture for over three years." His mouth quirked. "I'm free, unattached, uncommitted, and unmarried. Have dinner with me tomorrow."

Women would stand in line for an invitation of this sort. She felt the draw, the desire to say yes, felt the remnants of doubt and confusion. Hesitation made her speechless.

"Also, I'm impatient," he said lightly.

She took a deep breath, her mind dangerously giddy with new possibilities, new hope. "All right, let's have dinner tomorrow night."

"It's time for you to start seeing other men," Alice declared in her decisive-nurse voice. It was only moments after Aidan had left with his wallet and Alice had dropped by for a cup of coffee and to give Gwen a book she'd asked to borrow.

Gwen raised her brows at her as she switched on the coffee maker. "Oh, really? You think so?" She hadn't had a chance yet to tell Alice about Aidan's invitation and to ask her if she could baby-sit. Did Alice have some sort of sixth sense?

Alice had Churi on her generous lap and was absently playing with her bare little toes. "Yes, really, I think so," she answered dryly. "You've been hiding behind Joe long enough now."

"Hiding?" Gwen let her hands rest on the pile of freshly washed, sweet-smelling baby clothes she was ready to fold.

"As long as he's around, you can afford not to look at other men."

"Don't be ridiculous." The words came out a bit too quickly. Gwen focused her eyes determinedly on the tiny white shirt in her hands, knowing all too well that Alice was right. She'd just never really thought about it in those terms.

Alice scowled. "You're not in love with Joe, but you've shown no interest in seeing other men. You can't grieve forever, you know."

"Thank you for your wisdom, Alice," Gwen said mildly.

Churi gave a frustrated wail as she tried to squirm loose from Alice's arms. Alice handed her a toy, which calmed her for a moment.

"I know Marc was a real prince," Alice went on, her tone a little softer now, "but there are other special men out there."

"I don't doubt it, Alice." Gwen folded a pink shirt and put it on the pile.

"Marc would want you to be happy again, wouldn't he?"

Gwen nodded slowly. "Yes, he would."

Alice stroked Churi's soft, dark hair. "You're young. You need a man. You want children. So hurry up, girl."

Gwen laughed, she couldn't help it. "Where shall I start? The Yellow Pages? You make it sound so simple."

"It *is* simple. You're generous and loving, you're a wonderful teacher, you're smart and pretty and independent. You've got everything going for you. So what's not simple?"

Gwen carefully folded a flowered crib sheet. "Finding the right man is not simple. Falling in love is not simple. It doesn't happen on command, you know."

"It sure as heck won't happen if you're not open to it," Alice declared. "You're giving off all the wrong vibes."

"Oh, really? Tell me the vibes I'm giving off."

"You're standoffish. You might as well have a sign hanging around your neck saying *KEEP OFF*! *DON'T TOUCH*! *GET LOST*!"

Gwen laughed. "I must say, talking to you is very revealing, as always."

Alice gave a long-suffering sigh. "You're not paying any attention to what I'm saying, are you?"

"I'm paying lots of attention," Gwen said soothingly. "As a matter of fact, I'm going out to dinner with a man tomorrow night. If you can baby-sit."

"I can baby-sit."

"Thank you."

"Be careful, now," Alice went on, not in her nurse's voice but in her equally well-practiced concerned-mother tone. "There are lots of weirdos out there. You're sure this man is not a weirdo?"

Gwen groaned. "Alice!"

Gwen felt like a total wreck. It had taken her two hours to get dressed, trying on at least ten outfits. When was the last time she had ever felt this nervous and insecure? She couldn't even remember it. It had been years and years. It was pathetic. She groaned at herself and then laughed at her own folly.

Well, this would have to do. She looked at herself in the mirror, examining the slim-fitting black silk jersey dress, sleeveless and simple, nicely complemented with an exotic necklace of amber beads.

Her hair had a healthy gloss to it—like polished mahogany, as Aidan had once called it, and curled softly around her face. She looked elegant and sophisticated. In fact, she looked gorgeous, even if she said so herself. Confidence was good for a person, and she should know. There had been times when she'd had very little, and then she'd grown up and she'd cultivated some, and it was her experience that having confidence was a lot better than not having it. She picked up her brush and gave her hair a last touch-up.

She was ready when Aidan rang the bell at seven. She rushed down the stairs to open the door, finding that Alice had beaten her to it and was introducing herself while giving Aidan a thorough inspection with her sharp eyes.

Gwen stopped at the bottom of the stairs and stared as she took in the change in him. He wore a suit and a tie, he'd had a haircut and his chin was cleanly shaven once more. A storm of emotion rushed through her at the familiar look of him. He'd lost the slightly sinister look and he looked intimately familiar—like the Aidan from long ago.

His eyes met hers and he gave a crooked smile. "You keep surprising me. You look...stunning."

She swallowed. *So do you*, she wanted to say, but didn't.

She gave Alice some last-minute instructions, but Alice rolled her eyes and practically pushed the two of them out the door. "Go have some fun, and leave the baby to me," she said.

Aidan took her to a restaurant that had only recently opened and had been designed to look like a Swiss mountain chalet. Gwen surveyed the decor with interest. She'd never been here before, and she wondered if Aidan had chosen it because it would be neutral territory. No memories here for them, and she couldn't have been here with Marc, either.

She still felt uneasy at the thought of spending the next couple of hours alone with him—not sure what to talk about, what to say or not to say to him. He seemed perfectly calm and controlled and it annoyed her that she didn't feel the same, that her normal self-confidence somehow melted away in his presence. They ordered drinks and she became aware of a spark of amusement in his eyes as he observed her.

"What's so funny?" she asked, trying to sound light rather than defensive.

"It just occurred to me why you reacted with such prim and proper outrage when I kissed you. It was because you thought I was married."

Warmth suffused her at the memory. "I don't like married men who play around on the side. Or women, for that matter. I don't consider that being prim and proper. It's called having standards." She hoped she didn't sound too pious.

He nodded in agreement, the spark of humor still in his eyes. "I like people with standards. It's not comforting, however, to think you assumed I didn't have any, and that I was capable of being unfaithful," he said lightly.

The waiter came with their drinks. She took a sip from her wine. "I haven't seen you in twelve years," she said evenly. "I don't presume to know you. Besides, everybody is capable of infidelity. It's a matter of whether you allow yourself to commit it.''

He took a drink and observed her over the rim of his glass. ''You seem very confident.''

''About that I am,'' she said breezily. ''It's real easy.''

''You were never unfaithful in eleven years of marriage?'' he asked casually, putting the glass back on the table.

''No.'' It was the truth. Why then did she feel this faint uneasiness creep through her? She swallowed some more wine. ''Actually, that was rather a personal question, wasn't it?'' she asked.

He nodded. ''Yes, it was, and I do apologize.''

A loud crashing exploded into the quiet ambience of the restaurant. China shattered, glass splintered, cutlery clanged, a woman shrieked in surprise.

''Oh, no,'' Gwen muttered as she took in the disaster scene. A waiter had lost his balance and dropped an overloaded tray of dirty dishes on the floor between the tables. It was not a pretty sight.

Within seconds a rescue team was on the scene and the commotion was over in mere minutes. Gwen was sorry for the waiter, but not sorry for the distraction.

The drink was beginning to relax her a little. Over the appetizers, Aidan told her about Ella and the book they were writing. He asked about Churi and she told him her parents had walked and hitchhiked all the way from Mexico, all through California, to Oregon, where they had jobs waiting in a coastal resort hotel. The accident had happened as they'd almost reached their destination. By some incredible miracle, Churi had been unhurt. Like Churi, the parents had been weak and malnourished, which was complicating their recovery.

The main course arrived. Wine was poured. The smiling waiter disappeared. Gwen talked about her work and how much she enjoyed teaching small children.

"You went to college while you were married, then?" Aidan asked lightly.

She nodded. "Yes."

"How did you meet your husband?" Aidan concentrated on his steak as he spoke, his voice politely interested, yet she knew she did not imagine the tightness in his tone—faint, but real.

On a moonlit beach. By a mountain stream. On a Caribbean cruise.

"In a parking lot," she said. "In the pouring rain."

"Very romantic." A note of humor colored his voice, which was a relief.

"It was a lucky thing," she said lightly. "I was about ready to throw myself off the nearest bridge, if I could have managed to climb out of the bottomless pit I was finding myself in." She wiped her mouth with her napkin. "It had been one of those days," she added breezily.

He cocked one eyebrow. "I'm intrigued now."

"You want me to tell you the sorry details?"

"Every one," he said evenly.

"I'll be brief." She put the napkin back on her lap. *Just give him the facts*, she said to herself, *no emotion.* "It was the week after my mother died," she began. "The landlord had told me to get out of the house by the end of the week. I'd spent my savings for college on my mother's medical bills, and my car had just given up the ghost in a parking lot."

"One of those days," he said dryly.

"Yes. Just picture this. Here I was: motherless, penniless, homeless and carless. And out of the rain came this handsome stranger to my rescue."

That had been twelve years ago. She could be light about it now. It hadn't been funny then—the total despair, seeing no hope at all. Aidan gone, her mother dead, no house to live in, no college to go to and no car to drive in a place where there was no public transportation to speak of.

Marc had found her soaking wet, kicking the car, crying hysterically. Over the years the story had been embellished with more dramatic detail, creating a rather vivid image of her as a beautiful lunatic with wild eyes, kicking the car and raging at the heavens. Marc had loved telling it to their friends, all in good humor.

So what did you do? their friends would ask. Take her to an asylum? No, said Marc, I married her.

Which was about right. Three dizzy weeks later she found her circumstances changed dramatically. She was the wife of a kind and wonderful man. She lived in a comfortable apartment, while her architect husband was designing a dream house for them. She was enrolled in college and had a new car to drive. I'll pay you back, she'd said, uneasy with all his generosity, and he had laughed. You're my wife, he'd said. What's mine is yours.

His parents loved her. His friends loved her. He loved her. The world was suddenly a different place, a place of comfort and warmth and an abundant lack of worries. After all the stress and misery of the last few months, she basked in the peacefulness of her life. She could breathe again. She could sleep again. She could even laugh again.

Gwen wasn't ready to share all that with Aidan, so she speared a shrimp and smiled brightly. "So, tell me about your adventures around the world. Start with Rwanda. All I think of is jungles, gorillas and Pygmees, and I'm sure there's a lot more."

There was. She listened to him tell her about his work in the hospital, asking questions, and noticing how slowly his voice changed—from the cool and academic to the warm and enthusiastic. After five years in Africa he'd moved to Bangladesh, then to Ecuador. It was good to recognize the old, familiar Aidan again, to see the silvery lights back in his eyes.

Her nervousness disappeared magically. Time passed—exciting hours filled with new images and ideas, visions of another world, another life, new insights into the heart and mind of a man she'd once known so well. They talked and ate and laughed easily and it amazed her to find suddenly that hours had passed, that dinner was over, that she'd eaten a huge piece of chocolate mousse cake and that it was time to leave.

"Thank you," she said as they were driving back. "It was wonderful talking to you." As it had always been. He ignited in her a wonderful kind of excitement, a curiosity for new and interesting things, a need to explore thoughts and ideas and unknown places and people. He energized her, made her feel alive in mind and in body.

Arriving at her house, he parked the car and walked up to the front door with her, taking her key and putting it in the lock.

She did not want the evening to end. She wanted to keep on hearing his voice, seeing his face, feeling alive the way she was feeling now.

Would you like to come in for a cup of espresso or cappuccino? How easy it would be to utter those words, yet as she looked at his strong, brown hand opening the door, the beautiful, hand-carved door that Marc had brought all the way from Mexico, something inside her held her back, an undefinable emotion, a force she did not understand.

Marc would want you to be happy again, Alice had said. Of course he would have. She didn't doubt it. Yet her mouth would not move, not express the invitation to the man now standing by her side.

He smiled as he handed her the key. "Thanks for a very enjoyable evening," he said.

"Thank you," she returned, feeling all her confidence desert her. A breeze touched her heated face. Around them the air quivered with the nocturnal serenade of insects.

He reached out and took her face in his hands and looked into her eyes. Silvery eyes. Eyes with emotions she had not seen for a long time—emotions she had feared might not exist in him any longer. Their evening together had brought them out and they were there for her to see, to claim.

His hands were strong, yet tender around her face. Her heart thundered, blood rushed wildly through her and she couldn't feel her legs anymore. His mouth came down on hers, warm and full of passion, but the aching need inside her was over-whelmed by something else—a painful force fighting the yearning and hunger inside her. She strained against his hands, pulling her mouth away from his with an anguished little moan that seemed to echo in the darkness around them.

He let go instantly, as if he'd burned himself against her struggling mouth.

A moment of throbbing silence hung between them.

"I'm sorry," she whispered, feeling the hot sting of tears, feeling a deep grief of loss and regret, knowing not how to make it right.

"Goodnight, Gwen," he said, his voice un-steady, barely controlled. Yet what it was he was controlling, she could only guess at. No emotion in his eyes now. Whatever she had seen there had swiftly gone back into hiding.

"Aidan..." Her voice failed her and he did not hear her as he turned back to the car.

She moved inside and closed the door quietly. With her back against the wall, she dragged in a deep, steadying breath in an effort to calm herself enough to go in and face Alice's sharp, all-seeing eyes.

No worry necessary on that score. Alice was sitting on the edge of her seat watching the conclusion of a horror movie on television. She waved a hand at Gwen in greeting, her gaze riveted to the screen. With a sigh of relief, Gwen made her way to the kitchen and had a cooling drink of water.

After Alice had left, Gwen looked in on Churi, then went to her bedroom and sat on the edge of the bed, feeling dazed. What had happened?

She was falling in love with Aidan again, all over again. No, it was more than that. She loved him, she still loved him. It had never truly left her. Tonight she'd felt as if she'd found part of herself again, a part of her that had been lost. A wonderful, exciting part that made her feel vibrant and exhilarated.

She took a pillow and hugged it against her chest. So why hadn't she wanted him to kiss her? What had made her draw back from him? What were those awful, anguished feelings hiding in the background—feelings she did not want to name?

She looked at the picture of Marc on the bedside table. Warm brown eyes smiled at her. Tears flooded her eyes, blurring his smiling face. Her arms tightened around the pillow.

"I'm sorry," she whispered. "Oh, Marc, I'm so sorry."

"Is he a good guy?" Alice asked the next morning over the phone.

"Yes, he's a very good guy." Gwen spooned baby cereal into Churi's mouth with her free hand.

"Does he treat you right?"

"Yes, he does."

"Good. That's the most important."

Gwen couldn't help smiling. ''What comes after that?'' Alice was looking after her, and it wasn't a bad feeling. She'd met Alice in the hospital when Marc had died and Alice had taken her under her motherly wings and been a part of her life ever since. Gwen loved Alice. Gwen needed Alice. Her down-to-earth advice, her positive attitude had very restorative powers.

''Personal integrity and a sense of humor,'' Alice informed her promptly. ''Does he have those?''

''Yes.'' Gwen grinned into the phone. ''And then?''

''Why are you smirking?''

''I'm not smirking. You can't even see me. I'm just wondering when you're going to ask me what kind of job he has and if he makes lots of money.''

Out of the past came her mother's face, her mother's voice.

Clear, vivid.

''You're sure cheerful these days,'' her mother said, scooping up another serving of instant mashed potatoes. ''You've got a boyfriend?''

Gwen looked down at her plate and bit her lip. Boyfriend. Aidan was not a boy. He was a man. ''Not really,'' she said, and her mother laughed.

''Then what?'' She pushed a lock of graying hair behind her ear. She didn't look well. There was a dull cast to her skin.

Gwen swallowed, feeling torn. One part of her wanted to tell her mother and share the wonderful way she felt, share the joy. Another part wanted to keep it a secret. Her love for Aidan was something precious, a tender, fragile thing. Her mother wasn't very good with tender, fragile things.

"He's not a boy, Mom. He's older," she said.

"Older? How much older?" Her mother lit a cigarette and gave her a suspicious, narrow-eyed look. Gwen knew the ideas going through her mother's mind and felt her heart sink.

"Nine years. He's twenty-seven."

"Does he have a good job? Does he make decent money?"

Her heart sank a little further. "He has a wonderful job, Mom. Do you want some more peas?"

Her blatant attempt at changing the subject was not successful. She hadn't had much hope.

"What kind of job?" Her mother blew smoke up into the air, her eyes not leaving Gwen's face.

"He's a doctor, a pediatrician. He works at the hospital."

Silence. Her mother looked stunned, but quickly recuperated. "A *doctor*? Good God, where did you find a *doctor*?"

"In the hospital." Gwen gave an hysterical little laugh. "He's a wonderful man, Mom."

"I'll bet," her mother said dryly, a wealth of meaning in her tone. She tapped ashes onto her plate where they landed on a bit of cold mashed potatoes. She gave a frustrated sigh. "Where are your brains, Gwen? What would a *doctor* want with a girl like you?"

Gwen took a deep breath and shook her head clear of long-ago voices and images. Over the phone, she heard Alice's indignant exclamation. "I was going to ask you no such thing! As long as he isn't a pyromaniac, a drug dealer, a serial killer, or a professional gambler, I don't care what he does for a living. As long as he's a decent human being without a criminal record.'' She'd given this speech to several daughters and Gwen sensed that there was more along the same lines.

''As a matter of fact, he's a doctor, a pediatrician. Is that all right?''

Apparently there was some doubt there, since a short, pregnant silence followed her words. As a nurse, Alice had strong feelings about doctors, not always positive. ''Who?'' she asked, a threat in her voice. It would not do to go out with a physician on Alice's black list.

Gwen wiped cereal off Churi's nose. ''You don't know him. He's worked overseas for the past twelve years. His name is Aidan Carmichael.''

''I know the name. Why do I know the name?''

''You may have heard about him. He's well-known in tropical medicine. He won some big award.'' Gwen went on to tell Alice about Aidan's work in developing countries, his research, his book, whatever she knew about Aidan's illustrious career.

''I hope he deserves you,'' Alice said.

''I have a problem and I'm looking for inspiration,'' said Aidan. ''I wonder if you could help.''

He stood on her doorstep, a bundle of paper in his hands, and he was all business, which was a relief of sorts. He gestured back over his shoulder, toward the shiny red Mazda on the driveway, the new car she had bought that morning bearing temporary tags. "You have company? I won't keep you."

"No, no. That's my car. I sold the Porsche."

His brows shot up. "Really? Why?"

She shrugged. "This is more practical." Which was true. She'd chosen red for the color again—it was a passionate, optimistic color and she liked it.

His eyes narrowed a little as he surveyed her face, but he made no comment. She wondered what he thought, and why it should matter. Did he see her as a spoiled, rich woman? Well, maybe she was, in a way, but she'd always had a little trouble really seeing herself as such—in spite of the nice clothes and big house and fancy car she owned. She enjoyed it all, yet something elemental inside her had never really changed from the person she had been growing up in a shabby little house with few material possessions. Luxuries were nice, but happiness didn't come from having nice things.

She hadn't heard from Aidan for a couple of days after he had taken her out to dinner and every time she thought of how she had refused his kiss, her stomach twisted into painful knots.

Her stomach was twisting into knots now as she stood there looking at him standing in her doorway, and she felt an overwhelming need for him to understand, to know—only she wasn't sure what exactly that was, and how she could possibly even explain it to him if she didn't understand it herself. Her hands were clammy and she slid them surreptitiously over the seat of her denim shorts.

"Gwen?" He looked at her, brow raised in question. "May I come in for a minute?"

She stepped aside hastily. "Yes, yes, of course." Closing the door behind him, she leaned against it, hands behind her back, and faced him.

"I want to apologize," she said, hearing the nervous note in her voice.

"For what?" He searched her face. "For not wanting me to kiss you?"

"Yes, no."

"No need to, Gwen." He seemed perfectly controlled, his expression giving nothing away. "You certainly have the right to refuse to be kissed if you don't want to be kissed."

"That's not what it was, Aidan." Oh, God, why did she feel like such an idiot? Why did she feel as if she were eighteen again—unsure of herself, overpowered by his strong male appeal, overwhelmed by conflicting emotions she had no idea how to sort out for herself, much less explain to him?

She swallowed miserably. "I wanted...it had nothing to do with you or what I was feeling...for you." Her heart was hammering in her chest and she gulped in air.

"Joe?" There was a sharp edge to his voice.

She shook her head. "No. He's a good friend. We're not...involved, romantically, I mean. It was something else." She shrugged helplessly. "It was me. I...I don't know."

"It's all right, Gwen. I'll live." His tone was light now, his face smooth.

She wished she could tell what he was thinking, but it was impossible. Apparently his male ego had not been damaged too severely, because here he was, asking for her help.

The very thought of damaging Aidan's male ego almost made her smile. He had an ego of cast iron; it was damage proof. Or so it had always seemed to her when she was younger. She wasn't so sure now. There was more to his cool, confident manner than met the eye.

She moved away from the door, forcing herself to be calm. "What kind of help do you need? You want a cup of coffee first?"

He followed her into the living room. "No coffee, thanks. I'm on my way into town and thought I'd check with you if you had any ideas." He tapped the papers in his hand. "I can't find a file in my computer or on a disk anywhere for this material. I suppose it's on a disk still in Ecuador."

"Sit down," she said, waving at a chair.

He sat down, tossing the bundle of papers on the table. "It's Spanish and a copy of it is supposed to go to the translator in three days. As you see, it's a mess and I can't send it in like this. It has to be put into the computer and cleaned up. I need someone with enough knowledge of Spanish to be able to enter this in on short notice."

Gwen picked up the handwritten text. Lines and words were crossed out, corrected or changed. The handwriting was difficult to read, but not impossible. It would be an annoying job, to say the least.

"Have you tried the office services businesses?"

"Yes." He shrugged impatiently. "I have tried everything. The problem is the time frame. Nobody can have it done over the weekend and have it back to me by Monday night. I was wondering if you know anyone. A friend. A teacher on vacation. Anyone with enough Spanish knowledge to be able to type it in. It doesn't have to be perfect. Once it's on a disk I can clean it up myself. I just don't have time to enter it.''

The solution was simple, of course, she knew. She could do it. Marc's computer was upstairs, in his office. It would take some time, but she could do it.

If she wanted to.

She looked down at the messy text. ''I have an IBM computer. I can handle WordPerfect, I know enough Spanish, and I can make time.''

A short silence hummed between them. ''That meets all the requirements and qualifications,'' he said slowly. He held her gaze. ''Would you please do this for me? Set your price. Anything.''

''I'll do it, but I don't want to be paid.''

A dark brow shot up. ''It's a job. Why not?''

''It's all for the good of children, isn't it? I don't need money. If you insist on paying, you can make a donation to the hospital in Ecuador you're working with, or to the Migrant Laborers Children's Fund, or something like that.''

He nodded. ''It's a deal.'' He pushed himself to his feet. ''Thank you.''

A few moments later he was out the door again. She realized her heart was still beating erratically and her body was tense with nerves. Picking up the stack of paper, she glanced at it again. Churi was having her nap; she might as well get started right away.

He called her late Sunday afternoon. "How are you doing?"

"Fine. Typing. One hundred two pages down. I'll get it done by tomorrow afternoon."

"Fast work. You have no idea how much I appreciate this."

"No problem. By the way, this isn't your handwriting, is it?" She remembered his as being big and bold—not at all the handwriting of a doctor. This was small and squiggly and it was driving her crazy trying to decipher it.

He laughed. "No. It's my Ecuadorian research partner's." A slight pause. "Ready for a dinner break?"

"I need to feed Churi in a little while, and then I'll eat."

"Don't bother to cook. I'll get some dinner and bring it over. I need a break myself. I'm dead."

She stared at the keyboard. "Feeding me is not part of the deal."

He laughed. "It's the least I can do. Need to keep you in shape with lots of energy so you don't collapse on the job before it's finished. So, what do you like? Italian? Chinese? Hamburgers?" A fraction of a pause. "Mexican?"

"Chinese," she said.

"Anything in particular you like?"

"I like everything; you choose." She closed her eyes, seeing him in her mind's eye, knowing he would be with her not long from now and she felt her body reacting with a wonderful tingling sensation. He hadn't had to call, didn't have to come, but he was on his way. She felt a light sense of exhilaration and she smiled at her own excitement as she put down the phone.

He arrived an hour later and they sat at the kitchen table eating the food and drinking a glass of wine she had poured. Aidan held Churi on his lap and she fit there comfortably and was happy with his attention. He even managed to make her laugh. She felt safe with him. Gwen watched the big man and the little baby, feeling a softness spread all through her.

"She doesn't like strangers very much," she said, "but she's taking to you."

"A lot of babies don't like strange people at this age. They're starting to differentiate more and recognize familiar and unfamiliar faces."

"She recognizes her parents when we visit them in the hospital. She didn't see them for a while, when they were too sick."

"Does it upset her at all to see them? Or to go back with you after the visits?"

Gwen shook her head. "No. I was worried about it, but I think she's comfortable with me."

"She knows you love her."

Gwen watched him, images welling up from deep and hidden places in her mind. Images produced by fantasies and dreams that had never come true, yet had been engraved in her mind as if they were reality.

"I thought you'd be married, too, and have children," she said, her voice a little unsteady. "Why didn't you and Sophie get married?"

He shrugged. "It didn't work out that way." His voice was flat. "She had other plans and marriage wouldn't have been the right thing for us."

Gwen pushed around a shrimp with her chopsticks. "I see," she said, not seeing anything.

When they'd finished eating she put Churi to bed and asked Aidan to come to the office. She had some questions about some of the material she was working on.

He glanced around the large, well-lit room, a question in his eyes. All the paraphernalia of the architect were still there—drawing boards, big tables, along with all the standard office furniture.

"My husband's office. I . . . left it the way it was. I wasn't sure what to do with his things." A moment of awkwardness. She smiled and picked up the printed pages of the finished work. "I thought you might want these now to go over them even though I haven't finished everything yet."

He nodded and took the stack of papers from her, his eyes perusing the photos on the wall—photos of houses Marc had designed.

"He must have had a successful career," Aidan commented.

"Yes."

He glanced back at her. "Did he always work at home?"

She nodded. "Yes. This was his only office."

Hands in the pockets of his cotton Dockers, Aidan moved over to a large photograph of a massive Mayan ruin in Mexico. Gwen sat on a rock in the foreground, facing away from the camera, hair lifting in the breeze.

"That's you," he said. "Is this in Mexico?"

She nodded, feeling her stomach churning with sudden apprehension. "Marc's parents were born in a village nearby this ruin, in the Yucatan. They came to the States in the fifties, but they've kept contact with a lot of their family. Strong ties, you know. We went to Mexico often."

"Your Spanish is very good. I heard you on the phone the other day."

Talking to her mother-in-law. "I've had a lot of practice." So polite, so calm her voice sounded.

"Where else have you been?" His tone was light, too light.

"The east coast, Europe." She swallowed, fighting an intangible apprehension. "We spent several months in Italy and Greece and Spain. Marc loved seeing all the old architecture."

"Did you enjoy traveling?" A casual question, yet the air was thick with tension now. He thrust his hands into his pockets. They were balled into fists. Her heart lurched at the sight of them.

"Yes. I like traveling and seeing other places, seeing how other people live—the food, the houses, the music, the rituals." She bit her lip, afraid she'd said too much already, afraid of the turbulent undercurrents of the seemingly calm conversation. Damn, why had he asked?

"Traveling broadens your mind." His voice was flat. "It broadens your view of the world and your own life."

"Right," she said tightly. "I've broadened a lot in the last twelve years."

His eyes looked a stormy gray. "I'm glad you feel that way." Bitterness in his voice now, and an unmistakable anger.

She crossed her arms in front of her chest and hugged herself protectively, saying nothing, wishing desperately they could change the subject.

He met her eyes. "When you were in Spain," he went on speaking with slow determination, "did you learn to enjoy paella?"

Her heart slammed against her ribs and anger rushed to her head. No innocent question, this. Instinctively, she took a step back, her body tensed as if ready to fight. She glared at him. "What the hell is the matter with you?" she demanded. "If this is not a good subject of discussion, then don't ask the questions, all right? If you don't ask the questions, I won't need to answer them!" She dragged in a steadying breath. "But since you asked: Yes, Aidan, I've learned to eat paella—snails and all!"

CHAPTER FIVE

HE STARED at her, his face grim, his jaw like steel. "*I* wanted to show you the world, dammit!" he said roughly. He took a step toward her, taking his hands out of his pockets. He put them on her shoulders and looked into her eyes. "*I* wanted to show you the world!" he repeated. "I wanted to open your eyes. I wanted for you to take off your blinders, to see there was more than that narrow little world your mother offered you, that narrow little world she insisted you accept—no hopes, no dreams, no expectations. She kept you shackled to her own needs, for her own purposes. She kept you back from growing and exploring and experiencing life for yourself. She had no right!"

Gwen wrenched herself free from his grasp. "Don't!" she said fiercely. "Don't you dare criticize my mother!"

He shoved his hands back in his pockets and gave her a hard, silent look that spoke volumes.

Her knees were shaking and she clenched her hands so hard, her nails dug into her palms. "My mother did the best she could," she said, trying with all her might not to shout at him. "She was not a bad person, just somebody who got trapped and was victim of her own experiences."

His eyes were like a stormy winter sky—angry, cold. "She had no right to keep you from doing what you wanted to do, to manipulate you into staying with her!''

"She did it to protect me.''

"*Protect* you? From *me*?''

"From disappointment, from things going wrong.''

"Why did she think things would go wrong?'' Anger and contempt flashed in his eyes.

Her stomach churned with anxiety, a mishmash of feeling twisting and turning. ''Because they went wrong for her! My father walked out on her when she was pregnant with me, you know that!''

Her father had been restless, had Gypsy blood. He'd played the drums in a small band and traveled the clubs. Her mother had traveled with him for a while, then when she'd found herself pregnant, he'd left her.

Gwen tightened her arms in front of her, looking hard into Aidan's face. ''She woke up one morning in a motel room somewhere, and found him gone. She couldn't even remember where she was! He'd left a ten dollar bill on the dresser and a note, saying, *Sorry, kiddo, but this isn't gonna work*.''

"And she thought I'd do that to you,'' Aidan stated frigidly.

Gwen tried to relax her tensed muscles, willing herself to stay calm. ''She did the best she could, Aidan. I made my own decisions in the end.''

His mouth curved bitterly. ''You did?''

"Yes!''

"Then why didn't you come to Africa with me?''

She closed her eyes, fighting the onslaught of old memories and feelings. ''I was so afraid, Aidan.''

"Afraid of *what*, for God's sake? *I* was going to be with you!"

Her stomach clenched into a hard ball. Her heart began to race as if the old fear was still real, still had power over her. "I had awful dreams, terrible premonitions," she said shakily. "I didn't understand the meanings—just that I felt this terrible fear." She met Aidan's eyes. "I didn't know at the time, but I know now why that was, Aidan. I understood it later."

"And what did you understand?" He sounded skeptical, as if he didn't think there was anything at all to understand apart from the obvious.

She looked straight into his eyes. "On some intuitive level I must have known my mother would need me. Not because she said she did out of selfishness, or misguided protectiveness, but because she would get sick and die." She swallowed. "It was all very confusing at the time because I was scared of so many things—living in Africa, and all that, but I could have done that, I think, had I not felt that other fear that I didn't understand. I've often thought about it, and I know that's what it was—a premonition about my mother dying."

He studied her face for a silent moment, as if he made an effort to digest her words. "Tell me something," he said slowly. "If you were in so much trouble after your mother died, why didn't you let me know? Why didn't you write me, send me a telegram?"

She shook her head helplessly. "Everything went so fast, and I had no idea how to reach you. You were so far away—Africa to me was like another planet. It didn't seem realistic you could do anything, besides..." she swallowed at the sudden lump in her throat, "besides, I thought it was all over between us after what I said." Her heart contracted at the memory—painful even after all these years.

I don't love you! I don't love you!

"So you married him," Aidan said harshly, "three weeks after you met him in a parking lot." It sounded tawdry and cheap and everything inside her rebelled at the contemptuous tone in his voice. She stiffened in defense.

"I married Marc because he was good and kind to me! Because he asked me!" She clenched her teeth, feeling herself begin to tremble. "I was so far down, I saw no other way out. I was only eighteen, Aidan. I'd been taking care of my mother for several months until she died. I had lost everything. I had no place to live, no money, and no one to turn to. I needed someone to care about me, to boost me up, and he was there. He was the only one I could turn to, the only one who cared about me."

She saw his body turn to steel, saw the hard, angry line of his jaw. She saw him swallowing words.

She gulped in more air. "Maybe that sounds wrong. Maybe I should have been stronger, but I was young and inexperienced and he offered me a haven. It's what I needed at the time and I'm not sorry I did! Marc loved me! We had a good marriage and we were happy!" Her knees were shaking so much, she was afraid she wouldn't be able to hold herself up. She grasped the high back of

Marc's leather desk chair, taking in a steadying breath. "I'm not going to lie," she said, hearing the desperation behind the determination in her voice.

Aidan's eyes were the color of lead and his face was carefully expressionless. "I wouldn't dream of asking you to lie about that wonderful husband of yours," he said flatly.

Her fingernails dug into the soft leather of the chair. She fought for composure. "You know what, Aidan? I don't have to account for my marriage to you, or anyone else."

Aidan's face was carved out of granite. "Then, by all means, don't."

In the painful silence, they faced each other, the air alive with emotion.

She looked at his hard face, the face that could be so full of love and tenderness, the face of the man she had loved more passionately than she had ever thought possible. Again grief and regret overwhelmed her, washing away the anger.

"I take responsibility for things not working out between us," she said thickly. "But I cannot regret being here for my mother when she needed me. I know I hurt you and I'll always regret that. I know how cliché it all sounds, but I don't have better words. I don't know how to make you understand."

It had taken a long time for she herself to understand, and to accept that life did not always give you what you asked for and wanted with all your heart. It had been a long, painful process, but she'd made peace with herself in the end.

And now Aidan was back in her life, stirring up old memories, feelings, passions. She bit her lip and glanced outside, at the calm blue sky. A bird warbled a lovely song in the still air.

"It's a long time ago," Aidan said finally, as if dismissing the entire conversation, the past, the feelings. He seemed cool and calm again, as if his emotional outburst had never happened.

"Yes." Relief washed over her. She searched for something else to say, not sure where to go from here, but nothing came into her mind.

Aidan rubbed his chin. "What was it that you wanted me to look at?" he asked.

She moved over to the computer and picked up two of the handwritten pages, grateful for the excuse to focus on something else. "I'm not sure what to do with this. I can't make any sense out of the way it's arranged."

He stood next to her. Close. She felt his nearness in every cell of her body—a heightened physical awareness that made her feel light and trembly, as if her body knew all the memories that lay deep inside her, remembered the old feelings with a clarity as if no time had passed.

His hand touched hers as he took the pages from her and all her nerves danced with static. In that one instant, the tension was back, a different tension this time, not caused by anger and hurt. A tension that shivered through her every cell and made the air around them vibrate with its intensity.

She ached with the need to have him touch her, kiss her, to forget the past and all the pain, to make right what had gone wrong. She wanted back the magic of long ago.

Her hand shook. She saw him look and she clenched it into a fist and pushed it into the pocket of her shorts. He held her gaze, and she saw in his eyes the reflection of her own feelings—the old hunger, the deep need struggling for air and recognition. For fulfillment.

In the silence she heard the thumping of her heart, a deep throbbing that filled the air around her. "I...can't read this." Her voice barely a whisper. She tried to look at the page in his hand, but couldn't pull her gaze away from his eyes and the dark, smoldering fire inside.

From the corner of her eyes, she saw the paper slipping from his fingers and fluttering to the floor. The next instant he wrapped her up in his arms with a groan and his mouth found hers. She was lost, stunned by the fierce need of his kiss, the drunken dance of desire rushing through her, the abandon of her response to him with her own mouth and body.

A hurricane of emotion swept them away into a turmoil of desire that knew no time or place—until suddenly sanity returned. He let go of her, stepping back like a man in a trance, his eyes unfocused, his chest heaving.

Gwen sank down into the desk chair, feeling like she had no bones left in her body. She was shaking, struggling for air.

He wants me, she thought dizzily, and the very idea sent new heat through her. She couldn't stop trembling, knowing she wanted him, too, wanted to reclaim what she'd thought lost to her forever.

She saw the struggle in him, the fight for composure. He glanced around the room with what seemed to be deliberate intensity. His eyes turned the color of slate, and his jaw tensed into steel.

"I'd better go," he said roughly, turned and was gone.

Later that night she lay in bed wide-eyed, unable to sleep, Aidan's voice ringing in her mind over and over again. *I wanted to show you the world.*

Once he had offered her the world and she had rejected it. Memories came flooding back—images and words she'd hidden and tried to forget.

She'd come to the summer house in her mother's battered little car and Aidan had come rushing out of the door, waving a letter, looking excited.

"I've got it!" he called out, as he hugged her hard. "Just what I wanted and sooner than I thought. They want me in Rwanda, in Africa. A World Health Organization Project. It's perfect!"

Her heart gave a sickening lurch. "When will you go?" she asked, hearing the odd, toneless sound of her voice, feeling a cold fog of despair settling over her. So soon, so soon.

He looked at her, eyes wide, then took her hands. "Oh, Gwen, I'm not leaving you! We're both going! We'll get married as soon as we can."

She stared at him speechlessly. She hadn't dared hope for marriage, or any kind of permanency for that matter. *Where are your brains? What would a doctor want with a girl like you?*

Marriage. Africa. Africa might as well be the moon. She'd never even been outside of Oregon, not even to California. Her mind went into shock. She couldn't think. It was too much all at once.

He laughed. "Don't look so terrified," he said. "It'll be a wonderful adventure. We'll go to Europe on the way. It'll be our honeymoon. I'll show you Paris and Rome and Athens. I'll show you the world."

Honeymoon. Europe. She swallowed, feeling dizzy.

She saw his grin change to a frown of worry. He stroked her hair. "Are you all right?"

"I don't know what to say," she whispered, "I hadn't expected this."

"You knew I was going overseas eventually."

"Yes. I didn't think it would come so soon. I just . . . tried not to think about it too much." She'd expected it to mean that he would leave, and she would stay. She wasn't prepared to deal with his departure yet. She'd pushed it away in her mind.

And now he was asking her to marry him and go to Africa with him. Africa.

He held her tightly. "I love you, Gwen," he said huskily, his mouth close to her ear. "You are the most wonderful thing that has happened to me ever. You know that, don't you?"

"I don't understand," she whispered. "I don't understand what you see in me."

He laughed softly. "I see a thousand things in you—love and kindness and generosity and unselfishness and a wonderful toughness. You're real, you're special. There's no artifice about you, no playing games, no ulterior motives. Everything about you is up-front." He paused. "You make me laugh. You make me feel loved. It's the first time ever I feel I can just be myself with a woman. The first time ever I feel that I'm loved for who I am as a person, not for being a doctor or coming from a wealthy family and having status and money. With you I feel so much peace, so much joy."

"I'm so confused," she whispered.

He laughed softly. "I'll un-confuse you," he said, and kissed her.

It took her two days before she had the courage to tell her mother.

"Aidan wants to marry me," she said, her eyes on her hands as she was washing the dishes in a sink full of suds.

"Did he say that?"

"Yes."

"So what are the buts involved?"

Gwen looked at her mother and frowned. "What do you mean?"

"He wants to marry you, *but* you're too young for him. *But* you won't fit in his family. *But* you're not educated enough. *But* it's not the right time for him. *But*—"

"Stop it, Mom!" Her heart was pounding with anger.

"You don't have to yell at me," her mother said mildly. "There've got to be some buts, you know that, don't you?"

"There are no buts, period." She took a deep breath. "He wants to marry me and then he wants me to come with him to Africa."

There was a stunned silence. Gwen kept her eyes trained on the soapsuds. Then she heard her mother laugh. It was not a nice laugh. "Oh, Gwen, you can't be that naive."

Gwen squeezed the glass in her hand so hard, it cracked. "What am I being naive about this time?" she asked, her voice tight with barely contained fury.

"Sweetheart, he's going to *Africa*. He wants a woman with him. For comfort and convenience. How many women moving in his circles do you think are gonna go for that kind of deal?"

Gwen watched the blood well up in a cut in her thumb where the glass had pierced the skin. Red blood. All she saw was blood.

She clenched her jaws so hard, her teeth ached.

Roller coaster days. Elation and depression, joy and anger, excitement and fear. She was a mess. She tossed restlessly through the nights, the darkness full of unknown terrors, her sleep haunted by nightmares.

I love him. He wants to marry me.

What about Mom?

Her heart would race and a strange panic would overwhelm her. *I can't leave her by herself*! *She'll be all alone*!

Africa. Fear swamped her and her hands would be clammy. Strange people, a strange language. Where would they live? What would they eat?

She'd never even been on an airplane.
She was so scared.

The next morning, Gwen awoke drenched in sweat,
hearing Churi cry in the next room. She shook out
her hair and massaged her scalp with her fingertips
as if to push away the darkness in her mind. The
room was bright with summer sunshine and through
the open window bird song wafted in on the breeze.

A new day. A glorious day full of promise. She
smiled and threw her legs over the edge of the bed.
The past was the past. She could not allow it to
have power over her present.

The phone call came at eleven as she was typing
away at Aidan's work. The social worker, full of
good cheer, saying Churi's parents would be released from the hospital the next day, earlier than
expected, and would move into a small apartment
in the coastal town where they both had jobs at a
tourist resort.

Would Gwen mind keeping the baby for just a
few more days? Until Churi's parents had settled
and gained some more strength? They were eager
to have her back, but had been persuaded to wait
until Thursday.

Gwen's heart lurched in her chest. Thursday. On
Thursday, Churi would be gone.

Three days. Three days. She stared at the computer monitor, seeing nothing.

Somehow, she managed to finish the typing job that
afternoon and she called Aidan on the phone as the
printer was spewing out the last pages.

"I'm done," she said in the most calm voice she could manage. "I'm taking Churi to the beach for a while and I can drop the disk and the printed copy off on the way."

She drove up the drive half an hour later and parked the car. With Churi perched on her hip and the box with the printout and the disk tucked under the other arm, she made her way to the back of the house.

Passing the open French doors of the living room, she saw Aidan working behind the computer. He was dressed in white shorts and a blue T-shirt. He looked up as he heard her footsteps and gestured for her to come in. She moved inside, depositing the box on the coffee table.

"Hi," she said, "sorry to disturb you."

"I needed a break anyway." He came to his feet, rubbing his neck and stretching. He glanced at the box on the table, then back at her. "Thank you for putting yourself out for me," he said. "It was not an easy job, I know."

"No problem," she said lightly.

"And you're sure you don't want me to pay you?"

She nodded. "Quite sure." Her blood was tingling. She felt oddly light. It was hard not to think of what had happened last night.

They faced each other silently, aware of the tension in the room, the memory of that devastating kiss. She was glad to have the baby in her arms. He came a little closer and she felt her heart beating faster.

He reached out and took Churi from her, holding her up a little and making faces at her. She promptly gave a delighted gurgle. She was laughing more and more lately, as if she had more strength for happiness now that her body was thriving.

"She's looking good," he said.

"Yes." Her voice sounded unsteady, and he glanced at her, raising a brow.

"Something wrong?"

A sudden lump lodged itself in her throat. "Social services called today. She's going back to her parents on Thursday." She swallowed hard. "I hadn't expected it to be so soon." She took Churi from him and held her, but Churi didn't want to be held. She squirmed until Gwen put her down on the large sofa, from where she beamed them a triumphant smile.

"She'll be all right, Gwen," Aidan said quietly.

"I know. Her parents love her and can't wait to have her back." A child-care professional had been teaching Juanita, Churi's mother, how to take proper care of Churi's health, what to feed her, what to do and not to do. A social worker would carefully monitor the situation and regular doctor's visits had been arranged. Gwen forced a bright smile. She was determined not to get maudlin. It wouldn't do any good. "I knew this was the way it was going to be. It's for the best, but I'll miss her. I couldn't help getting a little attached to her."

He gave a crooked smile. "A little attached. Is that what you call it?"

She glowered at him in silent warning, and reached for Churi who was trying to slide off the sofa. "Go back to work. We're going to the beach."

"Any objections if I join you in a few minutes? I've been at it since five this morning and I could use a swim."

"Of course not," she said lightly, "Churi will be delighted to have the company," she couldn't help adding with a sudden, fervent need for lightness and humor.

She saw a spark in his eyes. "And you? Will you be delighted to have my company?"

"Oh," she said breezily, "I won't mind at all. It'll give me someone to talk with—stimulate the brain. Small babies are so distressingly nonverbal, have you noticed?"

He gave her a long, silent look, and she bit her lip trying not to smile, while at the same time her heart was doing flip-flops in her chest.

"You're asking for trouble," he said softly. "Do you know that?"

She feigned innocence. "Because I'm looking for some stimulating conversation?"

For a long moment he held her gaze. "Go to the beach," he ordered then. "I'll be there in a little while."

"Yessir." She smiled sunnily. "We'll see you."

Sitting at the water's edge, she played with Churi for a few minutes, then settled herself on a big beach towel with Churi in her lap and fed her a bottle of juice. She hadn't had much of a nap and she seemed a little drowsy. Gwen strapped her into her baby stroller with a teething ring and she seemed content to just sit and chew. The little stroller roof kept her out of the sun.

Gwen pulled off the shorts and shirt she'd put on over her bikini and rubbed sunscreen into her skin. As she put the bottle back, she noticed Aidan coming toward her through the sand, and her heart leapt in her chest. He was wearing short, black swimming trunks and had a towel draped over one bare shoulder. He was well-muscled and brown all over—all irresistible male appeal. Her throat went dry.

She was suddenly aware of her own body, dressed only in a bikini, leaving very little to the imagination—a body that was more womanly, more rounded than it had been when she was only eighteen, a body whose every cell stood at attention, waiting for the man coming toward her.

He dropped his towel and sat down next to her. "Hi." His gaze swept over her discreetly, then quickly moved to Churi. "She looks lazy and comfy."

"She didn't have much of a nap."

He looked back at her and awareness shivered between them—awareness and memories of long-ago pleasures, of present desires. It seemed difficult to find air to breathe.

"I'll go for my swim," he said abruptly, and marched off toward the water. She watched him go, fighting her emotions. Clenching her jaws, she dropped her gaze back on her bag and fished out some sheets of paper listing the features of houses offered for sale and forced herself to concentrate.

It seemed ages before Aidan came back out of the ocean. Water dripped from his hair, down his chest. He rubbed himself dry with his towel and Gwen averted her eyes, focused on the papers in her hands, feeling the treacherous reaction of her body.

He lowered himself next to her in the sand, leaning his forearms on his knees. "Working?" he asked, glancing casually at the papers in her hands.

"No. I'm looking for another house to buy." She wiped a strand of hair out of her face. "These describe some that are for sale. I want something small and cozy."

He lifted a surprised brow. "First the car, now the house." He frowned, perusing her face. "Tell me if I'm out of order, but do you need money?"

"Money?" She laughed, shaking her head. "Oh, no, that's not why I'm selling the house." Marc had left her well provided for with a generous life-insurance policy, which she didn't need, having a job of her own, and the equity in the house.

"Then why are you selling the house?"

"It's too big, too . . . fancy. I don't feel at home there anymore."

"Why not?"

She shrugged. "I don't really belong in it."

"After twelve years you feel you don't belong? Are you saying you're still suffering from the wrong-side-of-the-tracks syndrome?"

How he had fought that one. It almost made her smile, remembering. *It doesn't matter where you come from*! he had told her angrily more than once. *It only matters where you're going*!

She shook her head. "No, it has nothing to do with that."

"Then why?"

She hesitated. "Marc designed it and had it built for the two of us, and with the idea we'd have a family." She forced a lighthearted smile and spread out her hands. "But here I am, alone, and without children. What am I doing rattling around in that big empty house?" She did not want his pity. Pushing her hair out of her face, she looked out over the ocean, feigning relaxation.

"Why didn't you have any children, Gwen?" he asked quietly.

Her heartbeat quickened. "It didn't happen."

"That's what you said last time. But why? Did you and your husband see a doctor?"

She grasped a handful of sand. She closed her eyes for a moment. "I did." She watched the sand flow out between her fingers and willed herself to be cool and clinical. "I went through all the tests. They found no reason why I should not be able to conceive."

"Did your husband see a doctor?"

"No, he didn't." She looked up at the sky, seeing clouds gathering, obscuring the sun, felt a darkness gathering in her mind. "And don't ask me why," she said curtly, "because I don't know." She felt angry. As if she had betrayed Marc. Marc, who had been kind and loving and considerate. Who'd given her a home, supported her wish to go to college and become a teacher. Who'd listened to her when she needed to talk, helped her when she needed help. Marc, who'd boosted her self-confidence.

Oh, God, she thought miserably, why don't I miss him more? Why do I think of him so little? Why do I feel so guilty?

She knew why she felt guilty.

They did not stay at the beach much longer. Between them the air was full of dark thoughts and uneasy emotions. The wind started blowing and it looked like rain. Aidan helped her pack up and carried Churi back to the Mazda and deftly strapped her into her car seat. He had not pursued the subject of Marc's not seeing a doctor—there was no need to, of course. It was perfectly clear what he thought, but he'd had the civility not to air his opinion.

The next few days went by in a blur and then Thursday arrived. Gwen was packing Churi's belongings in two bright-colored canvas bags and a big box. She'd come with almost nothing—she was leaving with a treasure trove of clothes and toys given to her by Gwen's friends. Churi was going back to her own father and mother, who loved her and couldn't wait to have her back. Gwen arranged several stuffed animals in the box. It was a happy day.

Why then did she feel this terrible sense of desolation? She'd known from the beginning that this was going to happen, that Churi would be in her care for a short time only. She'd been sure she could handle it.

"*I can handle it!*" she said fiercely. "I love her, and I was supposed to love her. I'll miss her, of course I will. It's normal, it's all right."

She met the social worker at her office, who took one look at Gwen and put a hand on her arm. "It's hard, isn't it?" she said softly.

Gwen's throat felt raw. "Yes, but it's for the best. I know that."

The woman nodded. "Would you just like me to hand her over, or do you want to do it?"

"I want to do it. It will make me feel better."

Juanita was crying as she took Churi in her arms. She looked at Gwen and gave a tremulous smile. "You will be in our prayers forever," she said in Spanish. "You are an angel from heaven."

Gwen had been determined not to cry, but she could not help the tears burning behind her eyes. From some unknown reservoir of courage, she managed to smile at the two happy faces of the parents, wishing them well, telling them it had been a joy and a privilege to take care of their wonderful baby daughter.

Once in the car she could no longer keep the tears in check and they ran silently down her cheeks. Driving on automatic, she made her way home, anguished thoughts twisting inside her head. *I can't do this again. I can't do this again. I can't take care of a child and love it and then give it up. It's too hard. I can't do it again.*

Aidan was sitting on the front porch, waiting for her. He took her in his arms and held her tightly, saying not a word.

Gwen closed her eyes, accepting his comfort. She was grateful for his silence because she could not have been able to tolerate it if he had said all the things she knew already: that she had known all along Churi would go back to her parents. That her parents were loving people. That Churi belonged with them. Or if he would say something about having other foster children, as if Churi somehow was replaceable. Aidan would not think that, not Aidan who spent his life caring for children. To him each one was unique, each one irreplaceable.

His comfort was like a balm. He stroked her hair, soothing the pain. All of him was strong and hard, yet his touch was gentle, and her body relaxed against him, soaking up the warm feel of skin, sensing the steady beat of his heart.

She calmed herself and gently moved out of his embrace. "Thank you for being here," she said thickly.

They went into the house. Some force made her move up the stairs to Churi's room. It was so empty.

The sweet baby smell still lingered in the room, an invisible presence. She wondered how long it would be there. She wondered if she would ever have the courage to take on the care of another child, love it with all her heart, and then let it go.

She stood in the middle of the room, feeling again a hot rush of tears. She took a deep breath and let it out slowly.

"I'm a good mother," she said huskily. "I know I am."

He smiled at her. "Yes, you are."

"I always knew I would be, but it's a wonderful feeling to have the reality of it."

"You have a talent," he said. "The most important talent in the world."

She fought for composure, wiping her eyes. "I'm sorry to be such a sentimental slob, but I'll be all right. School starts soon and that will help keep my mind busy."

He took her face between his hands, and kissed her. It was a tender, loving kiss that made her feel warm and soft all over.

He smiled at her. "Now, let's go for a long drive along the coast and then have some dinner."

They found a rustic little restaurant and had a delicious dinner while watching the sun set over the Pacific.

Afterward they took a long walk along an almost deserted stretch of beach, hand in hand. Her bare feet felt good in the sand, still warm from the sun. It was very peaceful. She felt a peace settle over her as she listened to the soothing rush of the waves, watched the dark sky studded with stars. They sat down, backs resting against the hard rock. Aidan put his arm around her and she leaned her head against his shoulder. It felt good and natural. She took in a deep breath of the salty air.

"It feels good to be here at night," she said softly.

"Yes. I like the beach at night. I always miss it when I'm gone."

Silence. Just the two of them in the dark. The sound of the sea. The sound of their breathing. The slow rise and fall of his chest. She closed her eyes, feeling a restless warmth suffuse her.

She wanted him so much, so much.

He shifted a little and lifted her face. His mouth was warm on hers, tender at first, then with a growing need, his tongue dancing with hers. Her body flared into full fire, her breathing grew shallow and she stirred restlessly against him. His hand caressed her breast, sliding over her waist, her stomach.

"I want you," he said huskily. "Oh, God, Gwen, I want so much to feel you again, to see you and touch you."

"Yes," she whispered.

"Come home with me."

"Let's . . . just stay here." It was hard to speak, hard to breathe.

She felt his smile against her mouth. "The animal in me would like nothing better," he said softly. "But it wouldn't be responsible."

Words and thoughts tumbled through her head, but stayed silent. He kissed her softly, then took her hand, jumped to his feet and drew her up against him, holding her hard against him. She buried her face against the warmth of his neck, the feeling of his hard body against every inch of her own, making her weak with longing.

She heard the pounding of the surf—an ancient rhythm, as old as time. She felt Aidan's hand closing around hers, strong, solid.

"Let's go," he said.

CHAPTER SIX

How they made it to his house, she had no idea. Her mind registered nothing but his nearness and the sound of his voice, as if she floated in some other sphere of consciousness where sensation was the only reality. In the bedroom he took off her clothes—quickly, kissing and stroking her skin all over, making every cell tingle with awareness of his touch. It was the most exquisite feeling to have his mouth and hands on her, strong yet tender, touching sensitive places.

His own clothes were gone quickly and they tumbled onto the big bed, breathless, aching, hungry. She kissed him, her hands roaming drunkenly over his body, over hard muscle and sleek skin and rough hair. She moaned into his mouth, the agonizing need almost too much to bear.

She'd had fantasies about their making love again, dreamed about it, yet nothing equaled the reality of the moment, the storm of feelings and sensations overwhelming her. She'd never known such hunger, such sweet, aching torment, and in a flash of rational consciousness she was aware of her actions, and the frenzy of her body.

Her body stilled. *I'm like a madwoman*, came the thought. She didn't recognize herself and for a moment a mixture of fear and embarrassment washed over her.

"What's wrong?" Aidan raised his head and looked into her face. She saw his eyes in the dim light of the moon spilling into the room.

She swallowed. "I . . . nothing. I'm scaring myself."

He laughed softly. "You're not scaring me. I love wild, honest passion." He put his mouth on her breast, teasing her nipple with his tongue. "But I have to admit, I don't remember you quite like this—all this wonderful abandon of yours is very exciting."

"You're embarrassing me."

"You're a grown woman. What's embarrassing about any of this?" His voice was soft. "It's magic. I love seeing you naked, seeing you move, seeing the desire in you. I love touching you and tasting you and feeling you against me." He gave a soft groan as he kissed her mouth. "And I'm going quite crazy with passion myself, in case you hadn't noticed."

She'd noticed. His words chased away her rational thoughts again, and his hands and mouth sent new sparks of electricity racing through her blood. She returned his kisses, her hands exploring his body, giving herself up again to the yearning that consumed her. Her body ached with a frenzy of sensation as his hands and mouth made music all over her body—dizzy, intoxicating music shivering through every part of her.

They kissed—deep, breathless kisses. They clung feverishly to each other, desperate for relief.

Her body reacted to ancient instincts, moved in a primitive dance of desire, arching against him, yearning for more and more. She heard the ragged sound of his breathing, the thumping of his heart against her own. She absorbed the sound, the taste, the feel of him deep into herself.

He said her name on a whispered moan, his control broken, and she answered him back on a shallow breath.

They moved in unison, tighter, wrapped together as one, arms and legs entwined, until the throbbing frenzy reached its peak and broke into trembling release.

Spent and tangled, they fell back against the mattress. Gwen held on to him, afraid to let go, afraid to lose the magic. Her heart overflowed with emotion—joy and gratitude and an overwhelming love—it was like something blooming inside her, something fragile and precious and exquisitely beautiful, something that could not be touched by words. She lay still against him, savoring the feelings and the languor stealing over her sated body. He stroked her hair, slowly, rhythmically, and she was grateful for his silence, grateful for his touch.

She awoke to his touch and joy rushed through her. She wrapped her arms around him and snuggled close as new desire warmed her blood. Through the open window she heard the chirping of birds and the rushing of the sea. Sunlight brightened the room. A breeze lifted the curtains and she smelled the salty air mingling with the scent of pine.

"You've changed in many ways," Aidan said softly. "But you're still generous and loving and unselfish, and I'm glad. You're a very special woman, do you know that?''

She laughed shakily. "You used to tell me that. I didn't understand it, but it made me feel wonderful just the same.''

"I liked making you feel wonderful, and it was so easy to do. You'd look so happy, like something blooming, if you don't mind me waxing poetic.''

"I like you waxing poetic.''

He kissed her tenderly, his hands caressing her breasts. "I'm thinking I was rather...voracious last night.''

She smiled against his chest. "Mmm.''

His hand teased her body. "I'd like to offer you a little more finesse.''

She closed her eyes. "Mmm. Show me.''

Soft little kisses—on her closed eyelids, her temples, her mouth. His tongue traced the edges of her lips, parted them, found her tongue. His hands were very gentle, teasing, tantalizing, finding warm, hidden places. She sighed. She felt wonderful—lazy, and still heavy from sleep. And a little guilty. She began an exploration with her hands, but he took them gently and put them on the bed.

"Just relax," he murmured. "This one's just for you. Enjoy it.''

In the end, of course, there was no way she could hold still. In the end she needed to respond—her mouth wanted to kiss, her hands to touch, her body move against his. Yet it all had a dreamlike quality—slow, sensual pleasure, intoxicating, dissolving in breathless rapture.

* * *

She missed Churi terribly—the feel of her warm, soft body against her breast, the solemn eyes, the precious smiles. Aidan's attentions made it easier—balancing out the sadness with the joy of rediscovering each other.

In the next two weeks, it was as if she could not get enough of him and he not of her. She stayed at the summer house at night, sharing the big bed, cooking dinner and breakfast for the two of them. When he went to work at his computer in the morning, she would go home, water her plants, prepare for the new school year and go out again to hunt for the perfect little house.

She loved him and hope bloomed inside her—a fragile thing surrounded by shadows. So many shadows.

She did not want to think of sadness and shadows.

Now that she was looking for a smaller house in earnest, it was time to become serious about sorting through the accumulated possessions of ten years of marriage. To sort through Marc's things. Six months ago she had finally had the courage to dispose of his clothes, but she had not yet gone through his office, mostly because she was not sure what to do with the things in there—business files, the blueprints, the technical books and other material related to his profession. Joe came to the rescue with the suggestion that some of Marc's professional stuff might be of use to university students. He made arrangements to have the desk, drafting tables, photocopier and other equipment moved and sold. On Saturday he came to the house, bringing an architect colleague of Marc's, and helped her sort through stacks of paperwork and files. It was an endless, boring job and she was grateful for their help.

The two men finally left late that afternoon, leaving Gwen with only a few drawers in Marc's desk to empty out and sort through. She was in the kitchen to get a can of Coke when the phone rang.

"How's it going?" Aidan asked.

Her heart made a little leap at the sound of his voice.

"I'm just about done. The men are gone, and the place looks really bare."

"Ready for some dinner a little later?"

"Absolutely. Somewhere bright and cheerful."

A short pause. "Are you all right?"

"I'm fine, just tired. If we go somewhere quiet and elegant I'll fall asleep in my soup. Very undignified."

"I don't want you to fall asleep in your soup. I want you to fall asleep in my arms, later, much later, after I've had my way with you."

She sighed dramatically. "You are so demanding, Aidan."

"And you love every minute of it," he said dryly.

"Well, I try," she said, and sighed heavily. "It isn't always easy though, I must admit."

"You're a little liar. It's always easy. It's always very, very easy. In fact you are the easiest woman—"

"I think you should stop right there."

He laughed softly. "You had it coming, sweetheart."

"You're going to pay for this. No one calls me easy and gets away with it."

"I can't wait."

"You'll have to. I want to get this done first."

"I find it very unsatisfactory to have this conversation on the telephone."

"Why is that?"

"Because I can't kiss you senseless. I can't get my hands on you. I can't take your clothes off. I can't touch you. I can't—" He heaved a sigh. "Shall I go on?"

She bit her lip. "Yes, by all means, go on." His words were having a disconcerting effect on her nervous system.

"I'll wait till later." His voice took on a crisp tone. "I'll control my frustrations until the time is right."

"Such a gentleman," she mocked.

"I'll see you in a little while."

She hung up the phone, smiling to herself, and glanced at her watch. If she hurried, there was time to get the job done before she had to shower and get ready for dinner.

The drawers contained mostly stationery, boxes of pencils and paper clips, and various office supplies. In the back of the bottom drawer she found a beautiful myrtle wood box, the shadings of colors ranging from pale blond to warm brown making an exquisite pattern. She had never seen it before and, trying to open it, she found the small lock closed. She looked around for a key, frowning.

Earlier this afternoon she'd seen a tiny key in the front drawer of the desk, somewhere amid a jumble of paper clips and coins and thumbtacks and rubber bands. She'd thrown it out.

Sitting on the floor, the smooth box in her hands, she felt a strange apprehension. What was in the box? And why was it locked? Why had she never seen it?

Marc had not been a secretive person, never hidden anything from her that she could remember.

She could force the lock open, break the box, but something inside her rebelled against the destruction. She'd have to find the key. She'd deposited the contents of the front drawer into a large plastic garbage bag, along with ancient business correspondence, old architectural magazines and an assortment of other junk. Rushing down the stairs, she put the myrtle wood box on the coffee table and went to the garage to retrieve the bag where Joe had put it next to the garbage can. She brought it back inside the living room and dumped the contents on the shiny wooden floor and sank onto her knees in front of it. Her heart was racing and she felt breathless, as if she'd performed a difficult physical task.

With trembling hands, she frantically began to search through the discarded junk, hoping desperately she'd be able to find the small brass key.

You're acting like a nut case, she told herself silently. *You're going to open that box and find high school memorabilia, or something equally innocuous. Then again, maybe it was a secret stash of ancient coins worth a fortune.*

After ten crazy minutes, she finally found the little key. She stared at it in her hand, her heartbeat going even faster. If only this was it—the right key for the lock. Reaching over, she took the box off the coffee table and inserted the key, or tried to. Her hands were trembling so much, it took her several attempts, but then it slid in smoothly and turned easily.

She lifted the lid. Her heart turned over. A photograph. Marc and a beautiful young woman, cheek to cheek, smiled up at her.

CHAPTER SEVEN

PHOTOS. Her heart gave a nervous little leap as she reached in and took the pictures out and found letters underneath, about ten or so, held together with a rubber band.

With a feverish haste, she looked at the other photos, several of the woman alone—close-ups that showed the happiness in her green eyes, the smoothness of her skin. Other photos of her and Marc together—sitting under a tree, arms around each other, standing by a barbecue, grinning at each other, a close-up of the two of them, cheek to cheek. He looked so young, so happy, so exuberantly happy, and with painful knowledge she realized that she had never seen him this happy, this in love— not in more than ten years of marriage.

She was shaking all over and the photos slipped from her hand to the floor. Picking up the small package of letters, she slipped the rubber band off, which broke instantly at her touch, brittle with age.

She opened the first letter and smoothed it on her knees. It took little reading, even with eyes blurred with tears, to know that it was a love letter, and she stopped after a few lines, skipping to the end. *I'll always love you, Julie.*

Julie.

She had never heard that name. She had never seen the woman in the photo.

Without conscious thought, she leaned over and took the telephone off the small side table. In a daze she punched in Joe's number, a separate, rational part of her wondering if he were home already.

He answered on the second ring.

She swallowed hard. "Joe, tell me about Julie."

Silence. She felt his shock all the way over the phone wire.

"How do you know about Julie?" he asked at last.

"I found pictures and love letters in Marc's desk. Who is she?"

"She . . . they were going to be married." He sounded agonized.

"What happened?" It amazed her to hear how calm she sounded.

"She died in a mountain-climbing accident," he said, and his voice sounded as if it took a terrible effort to drag out the words. "It . . . it happened a week before the wedding."

She closed her eyes and swallowed hard. "And when was that?"

"Gwen," he said gently, "I'll come back and we can talk about it."

"No." Her voice sounded like that of a stranger. "Just answer the question. When were they going to be married? Please Joe, just tell me."

"A couple of months before he met you," Joe said, his distress obvious in his tone. He knew what his words had to mean to her.

"I see." Her voice sounded oddly calm.

"Gwen," Joe said, "Marc loved you, you know that."

"Yes, I know that." She softly replaced the receiver and picked up the photo of Marc and Julie, cheek to cheek, love radiating from both of their faces. "You loved me," she whispered, "but never like you loved her."

She sat with the photo in her hand, tears sliding silently down her cheeks.

"Oh, Marc," she whispered, "why didn't you tell me?"

She didn't know how long she sat there with the letters on the floor beside her and the photo in her hand. She had no strength to move. All she could do was let the tears come and feel a sadness take over her mind and body, as if it seeped through her blood—a sadness not just for herself, but for Marc, for Julie, for all of them.

Somewhere on the fringes of her consciousness she heard footsteps on the stone terrace. Still she couldn't move.

"Gwen? Good God, what are you doing? What is all this junk?"

She looked up, lifting her head with difficulty. Aidan loomed over her, staring down at her surrounded by the contents of the garbage bag.

"Good God," he whispered. "You're crying." He sat down on his haunches beside her, seeing the photos, the letters. He picked up one of the pictures and stared at it. Then he took the opened letter and glanced at it quickly, then dropped it as if he had burned himself.

"Well, well," he said slowly, an odd, hard note to his voice, "looks like that perfect husband of yours fell off his pedestal."

She grew rigid, and for a moment she wondered if she hated him. "Shut up," she said hoarsely, wiping at her wet face. "Shut up, Aidan!"

He had the face of a stranger as he sat there looking at her. "Not a happy discovery to find that your man was unfaithful."

The fury she felt almost frightened her. "He wasn't unfaithful! And he didn't fall off his pedestal and he was a perfect husband!" She didn't care if she hurt him. "You know nothing about him, nothing!"

"I know plenty." His eyes were as raw as a winter sky. "You're determined to feel indebted to him for the rest of your life, aren't you? No matter what? You're going to revere him like some sort of infallible god who rescued you from a life in the streets!"

Every muscle in her body was strung tight. Anger was bitter in her mouth. "He never made me feel I owed him anything! Never!"

"He truly was a superior human being," Aidan said caustically. He looked pointedly at the letters and photos. "So what's this all about?"

"All this is from before we were even married!"

He examined the back of the photos for the dates marked on the paper, then dropped them into her lap. He pushed himself upright and shoved his hands into his pockets as he looked down at her. "So why are you crying?" The voice of a stranger. Detached, alien.

"I wish I'd known!" She hugged herself, shivering with unnamed emotions.

"Why?" he asked harshly.

She drew in a shuddering breath. "I was second best, and I never knew. I wish I'd known."

"Second best!" His voice chilled her. "Why in God's name would you have wanted your husband to tell you you were second best?"

Her throat felt raw. She swallowed with difficulty. "It would have made it easier for me." The words squeezed out with difficulty. She tried to swallow again. "I wasn't the perfect wife."

"Nobody's perfect, for God's sake!"

She closed her eyes. "I felt so guilty," she whispered. "I always felt so guilty."

"Why?"

"Because he was so good to me! He loved me, he was my friend. I felt inadequate because I couldn't give him what he deserved."

He pushed his hands in his pockets, his face a frightening mask of anger. "And what did he deserve?" His voice was frigid.

"He deserved for me to love him better!"

"You deserved for *him* to love *you* better," he bit out. "He denied you the possibility of children! He didn't even once see a doctor!"

"Shut up!" she said wildly. "Don't you dare criticize him!"

"I don't believe this," he ground out. He turned and slammed his fist against the nearest wall, then leaned his forehead against it and took in a ragged breath. Gwen saw him struggle for composure, struggled herself with the truth of his words.

Interminable moments later, he slowly turned back to her, looking at her with unreadable eyes. "What wasn't good enough about your loving?" he asked. "How did you want to love him better?"

She covered her face with her hands, wishing the tears would stop coming. *More passionately*, she wanted to say, but the words did not come out of her mouth, the admission too painful even now. Instead, she shook her head numbly, thinking of all the years of marriage, all the years of feeling she owed Marc more than she was capable of giving.

Passion. Had it only been lacking on her side? She struggled with the thought, the sudden realization, that perhaps it had not just been her as she had always assumed. She opened her eyes and looked at the photo. Perhaps the lack of true loving passion had not come from her side only—perhaps it had been lacking in Marc, as well. The girl's pretty face smiled up at her, radiating love.

She swallowed painfully. "He loved her," she whispered. "And he married me because he couldn't have her. She died a week before their wedding."

"And you never knew?"

"No. I never knew." New tears. "If only I'd known..." She reached for a box of tissues on a side table and wiped her eyes.

Marc had kept it from her. But she, too, had kept something from Marc. She'd never told him about Aidan. She hadn't wanted to hurt him. She bit her lip as truth dawned. Marc had not told her about Julie because he had not wanted to hurt her.

She could see the truth clearly now. She and Marc had been two people in pain and they'd given comfort to each other. It was all right. It was all right.

She felt a strange lightness, a dizzy sense of relief, as if some terrible weight had been lifted off her shoulders. *I'm free*, came the thought. *I'm really free.*

She carefully put the photos and letters back in the box and closed it, feeling a quietness inside her. She looked up at Aidan. "I'm all right now. I'll clean up this mess now."

Working in silence, they filled the plastic bag again with the discarded contents of drawers and file cabinets and Aidan put it in the garage.

He came back into the room and met her eyes. "I'm sorry for saying things that hurt your feelings," he said. The words came out with difficulty, as if he were struggling with himself.

She nodded. "It's okay. And I'm sorry you had to find me like this."

There was still a distance between them and she knew the last twelve years could never be wiped out or forgotten—she didn't even want to. They had been good years in their own way. Somehow the two of them would have to find a way to deal with the reality of the past, no matter how painful.

She moved toward the stairs. "I'll have a quick shower and get ready for dinner." She paused. "Actually, would you mind if we stayed here? I don't feel like going out."

A flicker of hesitation crossed his face. "Let's go to my place. I'll fix us something to eat there."

He didn't like being in her house. He'd never stayed the night, they'd never made love here. *Marc is dead, Aidan*, she wanted to say. *The house isn't haunted*. But she swallowed the words and just nodded. "Fine."

They cooked dinner together, not talking much, and ate on the large deck overlooking the ocean. She listened to the soothing rhythm of the water rushing onto the beach, over and over with each new wave. It was peaceful and calming and she was aware of a sense of freedom, of lightness, of serenity. On the fringes of her consciousness she was also aware of Aidan, brooding, not sharing her mood. She reached out and took his hand. His fingers curled around hers. They hadn't touched all night and the warmth of his hand gave her courage. She felt an overwhelming need to ease the tension out of him, to chase away the shadows, to show him she loved him.

"Let's go to the beach," she suggested. "Let's bring the wine, and a blanket to sit on."

A soft, cool breeze came off the ocean. They sipped the wine silently, looking out over the dark water, the white spume reflecting the moonlight as the waves broke. Gwen turned to him and put her arms around him and kissed him. He was completely still, and a shiver of fear went through her as she wondered if he might not want her close. The next moment he eased himself on his back and pulled her down with him. She went on kissing him, running her hands through his hair and down his neck and shoulders, filled with the need to relax him, to make him understand her feelings for him—

feelings that went beyond words, a truth of the spirit. Words would not be enough and she put all her love in her touch as she kissed him and pleasured his body with her hands.

He lay still, yet the tension did not leave his body—she could feel it permeating every muscle she touched. It radiated from his skin.

Then, abruptly, he turned, moving into action as he pulled her hard against him and kissed her with a hard passion, taking over the lead. His mouth and hands were all over her body, kissing and touching every inch of her until she began to feel herself dissolve into timeless, formless sensation.

Still, somehow, she could not quite let go. Vaguely, on the fringes of her consciousness, she registered something amiss, yet she could not put her finger on it, not identify the feeling. There was something not quite right, something about the intensity of his loving that she had never before noticed. She pushed the uneasiness away, holding him tight, letting the passion carry her away with him to a place where thought no longer mattered.

Afterward they lay side by side on the blanket, not touching. He said nothing and she remained silent, as well, not knowing what to say. She lay on her back and stared up at the sky. It wasn't the way she wanted it—this desperate coupling that had lacked any gentleness. It was clear to her now what had happened.

He'd made love to her as if he needed to show her possession, brand her with his body. She wasn't sure if she was angry or sad or afraid. Some dark shadow hovered around them, between them, separating them.

She buried the box of love letters and photos on Marc's grave and planted a rosebush on top of it. It was a sunny day, fragrant with the scents of clover and cut grass. Bees buzzed around the flowering bushes and white clouds drifted lazily in an endless blue sky.

She wiped the soil off her hands, still sitting on her knees and looked at the rosebush, smiling through a haze of tears. "I know you'll have found each other again," she said softly. "Be happy."

Slowly, she came to her feet and raised her face to the sun, feeling its warmth on her skin, feeling it enter her heart, filling her with peace.

Joe called her that afternoon. "Have you been in the bookstore today?" he asked.

Gwen's heart gave a little leap. "No. Is the book out?"

"Sitting in the middle of the store window in all its glory. They've made a huge display of it, with our picture included and a sign saying something about us being local folks. Looks fantastic." He gave a dry chuckle. "We may no longer be able to walk the streets unnoticed."

"I'm going out right now to look." Gwen felt a surge of excitement. The local paper had done an article on the two of them, and the story behind the book. Joe was giving a party on Saturday to celebrate the release.

"What did Aidan think of the book?" he asked lightly.

"He liked it. He was very impressed, as of course, he should be."

"Of course." A slight pause. "When is he leaving?"

"September."

"Are you going with him?"

Her mouth went dry. It was not a question she wanted to think about. "I don't know. We haven't discussed it." Her voice was businesslike, as if she were merely talking about a technicality that could be dealt with quickly and efficiently when they found some time.

She didn't feel nearly as confident as she sounded. Once Aidan had asked her to come overseas with him. Maybe he would not ask her again. Joe was asking a question she had not dared ask herself, eliciting thoughts she did not want to think.

Her relationship was so fragile—the feelings like tender seedlings that had long been denied the rain. So easy to destroy them, so easy for words to trample them.

There was another pause. "I don't want you to get hurt, Gwen."

"Don't worry, Joe. I can take care of myself." She squeezed her eyes shut, as memory rushed back into her consciousness. Her mother's voice, her mother's words.

I don't want you to get hurt, Gwen.

*   *   *

"What kind of place is Africa for you to be?" her mother asked, pushing her empty dinner plate away from her. She took a sip from the can of beer in her hand. "It's dangerous! Randa? I never heard of it."

"*Rwanda*, Mom. It's small. And poor." She'd gone to the library and found some books. She'd read about rain forests and gorillas and malaria, but decided it might be better not to mention this to her mother. It would not reassure her. It had not reassured her, either.

"You're out of your mind, girl." Her mother pushed the hair back from her face. It was too long, the perm had mostly grown out and there was a lot of gray in her hair. She was getting older. There was a waxy pallor to her face and she often seemed tired.

"And what about me?" she said. "What am I supposed to do?"

Gwen clenched her hand around her fork. Helplessness clogged her throat. She'd known it would come. She said nothing, staring at the food on her plate. She couldn't eat.

"You're all I got," her mother went on. "I don't want you going someplace I don't even know. Where I can't even visit you."

Guilt seeped through her. Oh, God, she didn't know what to do. "I'll come back, Mom. Of course I'll come back."

"I'll be lonely. You're all I got."

Gwen clenched her teeth, feeling a strangling sensation. She wanted to shout something angry, something terrible to hurt her mother, but the words got lodged in her throat.

Her mother lit a cigarette. "What you need is somebody reliable, somebody who can give you a decent house and some security. You don't need some Gypsy who keeps moving around and never settles down long enough to make a home with you. I don't want you to get hurt, Gwen."

Gwen dropped the fork on her plate. "Aidan isn't some itinerant nobody, Mom!"

"Like your father, you mean," her mother stated.

"I didn't say that!" Gwen waved a hand through the cigarette smoke to get it away from her face.

"Well, that's what he was. Oh, he was nice and charming and all the rest, but in the end, well, you know what happened to me in the end."

Anger and fear made a toxic mixture. "Aidan isn't him!" She was almost shouting.

Her mother made a grimace of pain and pressed an arm against her stomach. "Don't yell at me."

Gwen's heart leapt with fear as she looked at her mother's face going pale. "What's wrong?"

"Nothing, nothing." She pulled deeply on her cigarette. "Honey, you gotta believe me. You're too young to see down the road realistically. He's not the settling down type. How can you depend on a man who just wants to take off to some weird place and not even know how long he'll be there?"

"Mom, he wants to *marry* me!"

"Doesn't mean much these days, does it? So what if you get there and he decides he's made a mistake and he don't wanna bother with you after all? What if he leaves you? What are you gonna do? You got no money. He's just playing with you, girl. I don't want you getting hurt.''

''Mom, he's a doctor! He has an important job with the World Health Organization! He's *not* irresponsible!''

I love him, Mom! she wanted to add. *It's the most wonderful thing that has ever happened to me! He makes me feel good about myself, he makes me feel I am somebody. He makes me feel I am the most special person in the world.* The words stayed silent in her head. Her mother would only laugh—a mocking, bitter laugh Gwen could hear in her imagination.

She came to her feet, her whole body trembling. She couldn't take any more. ''I've got to go to work now,'' she said, and fled out of the house, away from her mother with her beer and her cigarette and her frightening words.

Aidan was in California for several days and she felt scared and alone. Courage came in momentary flashes, quickly doused out by fear, and the echoes of her mother's words.

It was all too strange, too frightening. Waking at night, she could feel the darkness strangling her, full of unknown dangers. She dreamed of steamy jungles full of monstrous insects and poisonous snakes.

It was a relief to be at the camp with the children and do familiar things—sing songs and swim in the pond and play with harmless frogs.

And then Aidan came back, buoyant, cheerful, carrying a dozen roses. He took her out to an expensive restaurant and suggested she try the paella. The restaurant was full of rich-looking people and she felt like Cinderella in her cheap cotton sundress. It didn't seem to bother Aidan at all that she looked like a poor waif. He never seemed to think she did, the way he talked, saying he loved the color of her hair, her smiling eyes, her kissable mouth, making her feel wonderful and strange at the same time. She wasn't used to hearing such admiring words about herself.

He ordered wine for himself and she asked for a Coke, embarrassed by the fact that she was too young to legally have a glass of wine with her dinner.

There were snails in the paella and as she saw them her appetite took a hike.

"You eat clams," he said, amused. "And oysters. Why not snails?"

"I'm *used* to clams and oysters," she snapped. "I'm sorry, but snails just don't do a thing for me." A wave of misery washed over her. Her hand trembled and she dropped her fork.

"No problem," Aidan said easily. "Order something else."

Tears filled her eyes. "I'm not hungry." She put her napkin on the table and came clumsily to her feet. Grabbing her purse, she rushed out of the restaurant. Hot tears ran down her face, cooled instantly by the wind coming off the ocean.

Aidan was with her moments later, putting his arm around her shoulders. "You're upset," he stated quietly. "I'm sorry."

"It isn't going to work, you know." She sobbed into his shirtfront. "I can't marry you. I can't come to Africa with you."

"Because you don't like snails?"

"Because I'm scared. Because I can't leave my mother here by herself. Because we don't belong together."

His body tensed. She could feel it. "And who the hell says that?" Cold anger in his voice. "Your mother?"

She drew back a little. "She's right, Aidan."

"She's wrong! All she sees is her own narrow little world and she sees it with a very cynical eye."

"I won't have you criticizing my mother!" she said furiously, stepping away from him, from the touch of his arms. "What do you know about her anyway?"

"I know what I saw the couple of times I spoke to her. I know what I heard when you talked about her." He shoved his hands in his pockets and looked at her grimly. "I haven't wanted to say this, Gwen, but I will. Your mother has a very negative view of life and she's keeping you back and holding you down."

"Shut up!" She whipped around and ran to the parking lot, realizing there was no way to leave but in his car. She had no money for a taxi and they were miles out of town.

He followed her and opened the door. She slid in, staring ahead of her as he settled himself in the driver's seat. She clenched her hands in her lap so hard her fingers hurt.

"I want you to take me home."

"First we'll talk."

"I don't want to talk." She sounded like a cranky child and it made her even angrier.

He said nothing and started the engine. He didn't drive her home, but took her to the summer house. She sat at the kitchen table in stony silence as he assembled a tray with grapes, apples, crusty French bread and various kinds of evil-smelling cheeses. He poured two glasses of wine, forgetting she didn't drink, didn't even like wine. She was too young for him; she didn't fit in his sophisticated world where people ate snails and moldy cheeses. She tried not to think about the food people ate in Africa.

He sat down across from her.

"I know you don't want to hear this, Gwen, but you can't have your mother decide for you what to do, and how to live. You're not thirteen. Parents are supposed to let their children go when they're old enough. You've got to live your own life, Gwen."

"I am living my own life!"

He took her hand and held it tightly as he looked into her eyes. "Then marry me and come to Africa with me."

Desperate fear and a dark sense of premonition clouded her mind. *What about me*? came her mother's voice. *I'll be all alone*. She yanked her hand out of his grasp and stumbled to her feet. "I can't, Aidan! I can't!"

He came to his feet, as well, his face working. "You don't love me." His voice was that of a stranger.

Her throat felt raw. Hot tears burned behind her eyes. "Don't say that!"

"It's true, isn't it? Just tell me! Tell me you don't love me!"

"No!"

He put his hands on her arms, his fingers digging in so hard it made her wince. His face was close, so close. "Let's just have it all over with, Gwen! Tell me you don't love me and I won't ever bother you again! Tell me, dammit!"

Anguish, fear, pain. She was shaking uncontrollably. "All right! All right! I don't love you!" Sobs racked her body and it was as if someone else were speaking the words. "I don't love you! I don't love you!"

Gwen found the perfect little house the next day. It had a wonderful view of the mountains and a wooded lot in back. A stone fireplace and old, well-polished wooden floors gave it a cozy, warm feeling. It had two bedrooms, a small, efficient kitchen, a bathroom, a nice living room—all she really needed. It was not far from the beach and not an unreasonable distance to school in town.

She was glad Aidan had taken off time to come with her. The house was empty. The agent was out of town and had given her the key to see it by herself.

"Nice little place," Aidan said, "but it's small and quite a change from what you're used to."

"It's perfect," she said. "I don't need anything more than this."

She didn't, did she? Why then did she feel suddenly so strange? This was what she had wanted. Exactly.

"You're very quiet," Aidan said as they drove back to town.

"I'm thinking. There's so much to do. I've got so much stuff to get rid of. I've got to put the house up for sale, too."

She'd decided to wait until she'd found another house to buy before selling her own. Her hands were clammy. She rubbed them on her jeans-clad thighs. Suddenly it seemed hard to draw in air.

Back home, Aidan followed her into the house. Gwen stood still in the middle of the living room, glancing around, taking in the familiar feel of it and suddenly, out of nowhere, an unaccountable sense of fear slithered through her.

She wandered through the rest of the house, taking in, as if for the first time, the bright, sunny rooms, the spaciousness. She looked into the bedrooms, walked downstairs again, feeling her heart begin to pound and pound and pound. A wave of panic made her body break out in a cold sweat. All she could think of was to flee, to run out of the house, far away from the unnamed terror that seemed to smother her and drag the air out of her lungs. She rushed out onto the terrace, sank down into the lawn chair, clutching her chest, gasping for breath, overwhelmed with raw panic.

Something was wrong with her.

She was having a heart attack.

She was going to die.

CHAPTER EIGHT

AIDAN was by her side instantly, reaching for her pulse. She collapsed against him.

"I'm ... I'm dying," she gasped, barely hearing herself over the thundering of her heart.

"You're not dying," he said calmly. "Try to relax and take in a slow, deep breath. Now, let it out very, very slowly. Concentrate on your breathing."

She tried to do what he said, aware of the feeling of his fingers on her wrist, the comfort of his presence.

"Good," he said. "Now sit up straight and do it again. Inhale slowly and deeply. Out, very, very slowly. Feel yourself relax." He took her hand and held it.

Slowly, fear began to flow out of her. She focused on the potted hibiscus with its big, exotic red blooms as she followed Aidan's coaching. As if by magic, she could feel her heart slow down, little by little, could feel calmness return.

She became aware of her surroundings again. Bird song. The scent of flowers. The sky, brilliant blue with white clouds floating in it. She followed the clouds with her eyes. It was very relaxing.

After a few moments she glanced back at Aidan. "I don't know what happened to me," she said unsteadily. "It was awful." She shivered, feeling the breeze cool on her wet skin. She looked down at her turquoise T-shirt, amazed to see it soaked through with perspiration. "Oh, Lord," she whispered, looking up at Aidan. "Whatever happened to me?"

"You were having a panic attack. Has anything like this ever happened to you before?"

She shook her head slowly. "No." Panic attacks were something she'd heard about on television or read about in magazines. "What's wrong with me?"

"Nothing physically. Your heart is fine. A panic attack is a physical reaction to stress."

"I'm not stressed! I was fine!"

He observed her calmly. "What were you doing right before it happened?"

"You know what I was doing. I was walking through the house."

"What were you thinking?" His voice was all clinical detachment. His eyes were cool, calm gray. She looked back at him, then broke away her gaze.

She slumped, closed her eyes. "I can't do it," she whispered.

"You can't do what?"

"Sell the house. I can't sell this house."

"Why not?" A simple question, yet his voice had lost its clinical tone.

She shook her head numbly. "I don't know." She balled her hands into fists in helpless frustration. "I don't know! I just know I can't do it, not now."

"Then don't sell it," he said flatly. "If you don't need the money, there's no reason why you should."

The voice of logic. She nodded. "I'll call the agent right now. I'll leave a message on her machine that I don't need another house anymore."

It was amazing how much better she felt having made the phone call. Aidan had gone into the kitchen and poured her a glass of water. They sat down again on the terrace.

"This is really weird," she said. "I mean, I don't understand how I could feel as if I were dying such a short time ago and now feel perfectly normal."

"The power of the mind over the body. There's a medical explanation involving body chemistry, if you're interested," Aidan said evenly.

"Whatever the medical reasons, I suppose it was a sign," she said. "I'm not meant to sell this house."

She glanced around the big, beautiful garden, the green lawn, the rosebushes. It took so much time to keep it all in order.

She sipped the cold water. "I don't understand it. I really thought what I wanted was a small house. I don't need a big house just for myself." She bit her lower lip, baffled by her own reactions. "I really thought I wanted to sell it."

"On a conscious level I'm sure you did. Maybe subconsciously, you didn't." His voice was even, his eyes devoid of expression. He took her pulse again. "It's back to normal."

She came slowly to her feet. "It's crazy. I feel fine."

"You are fine. Don't worry about it."

She smoothed her T-shirt. "I'm soaked. I'll go take a shower. Have a drink while you wait."

When she came downstairs, she found him sitting on the terrace where she had left him, staring out over the garden, no drink in sight.

They went out to a small Chinese restaurant and had dinner with old friends of Aidan's. It was nice enough, yet something wasn't quite right. Afterward, instead of taking her to the summer house, he took her back to her own house and walked her to the door.

"You want to come in for coffee?" she asked, and he shook his head. "I have some work to do tonight, so I'd better get back." He kissed her—a fleeting brushing of his lips over hers. She put her arms around him.

"Kiss me better," she murmured, finding his mouth and opening up to him.

He gave a soft moan in his throat, drew her closer against him and kissed her deeply, hungrily.

"Stay here," she whispered.

He drew in a steadying breath, and released her. He took her hands in his. "I can't," he said. His face was shadowed. "I'm behind schedule. I need a couple of days to get this section of the book finished. I'll see you at Joe's party on Saturday."

She nodded, feeling a constriction in her throat. Saturday was two days away. Hardly an eternity. Why was she feeling so strange?

"Is something wrong?" she asked.

"I'm just busy and preoccupied." He squeezed her hand. "I'll see you on Saturday."

She dreamed of children that night. Familiar faces—the children from her last school class, the children in the photos in the book, twenty, thirty of them, running through the house, sliding down the stairs, laughing, dancing, singing.

The next couple of days were hectic and confusing. People called to say they'd seen the book in the store, that it was wonderful, that they were buying it as Christmas gifts for friends. It was all a great thrill. Joe was ecstatic and Gwen found his mood contagious. The editor called from New York and asked if they'd decided to do another one.

The party was wonderful. Gwen felt like a celebrity, surrounded by admiring friends and assorted other people. And there was Aidan, looking very impressive in his suit and tie. He'd sent her a huge bouquet of flowers and a card, reading, *For the most talented and exciting woman in my life.*

When the party was over, late that night, they went to the summer house. She felt high with excitement and Aidan was amused by her enthusiasm, joining her in a mood of lighthearted fun. They made love outside under the stars, laughing and teasing each other. It was perfect. Perfect—except for the misty fears hovering in the hidden corners of her mind.

It was almost seven by the time Gwen arrived at the summer house on Monday. She parked the car and took out the grocery bag with the makings for dinner and walked around to the kitchen door. She heard the high-pitched shriek of sea gulls above the pounding of the surf. It was a perfect summer evening, the sun golden, the air filled with the scent of sea and pine trees. She took in a deep breath and smiled, feeling light and happy.

The door was open and she called out Aidan's name as she entered the kitchen. He wasn't there and she called his name again as she moved into the living room.

A suitcase stood in the middle of the room. She heard footsteps approach and Aidan came striding into the room, tossing a small carry-on bag next to the suitcase. His hair was disheveled, his eyes dark as if focused on something far and worrisome.

Her heart slammed against her ribs as she took in the scene. "Aidan, what are you doing?" A sense of dark foreboding flooded through her.

"I've been trying to call you for hours. You weren't home."

"I was at school for a planning meeting and then I went shopping. Aidan, what's going on?"

His expression did not indicate great and magic news. "I have to go back to Ecuador. It's an emergency. I'm leaving tonight."

"Tonight?" she whispered.

He nodded and raked his hands through his hair. "Two of my colleagues—they're a husband and wife team—have to go back to the States because one of their kids in college was in a serious car accident. He may not make it."

"Oh, how horrible," she said, feeling instant compassion.

He rubbed his neck. "With both of them gone, there isn't enough coverage in the hospital. I have no choice but to go back."

"No, no, of course not." The grocery bag felt like a ton of cement in her arms. *I've got to stay calm*, she thought. *I can't panic. I have to stay in control of myself.* She made herself take in a slow, steadying breath. "Shall I fix dinner?"

He shook his head. "No time. I've called for a taxi to take me to the airport. There's a flight to San Francisco at nine, and in the morning I'll catch one to Quito."

"Can I make some coffee, anything?" There was an odd sense of unreality about this scene and she fought not to give in to helpless confusion.

"Pour me a Scotch, will you? On the rocks." He moved toward the computer desk.

As if on automatic, she poured the drink and made her way back to the living room. She felt numb.

He was gathering papers, his face grim.

"What about your book?" she asked.

"Ella is coming on Friday to do some more work on it and the rest will just have to wait."

What about us? she wanted to say, but didn't. A flood of emotions washed over her. *Please say something*, she pleaded silently. *Please say you love me and want me to come with you.*

Aidan said nothing, sorting through the papers on his desk. The silence screamed in her ears.

"I'll come with you," she heard herself say. "I'll get ready and come next week."

He went very still. He did not look at her, his eyes focused on the files and papers in front of him. "No, Gwen. No."

Her stomach churned; fear did a mad dance in her head. "Why not?"

"This is not the time for this kind of decision. It wouldn't work."

"Why wouldn't it work?" She noticed the frantic tone in her voice.

He finally turned to look at her, his face oddly expressionless. "You don't belong in a remote, highland Indian town, Gwen. It's a bleak, poor, lonely place."

"You didn't worry about whether I belonged or not when you asked me to come to Africa!" she said heatedly.

"That was a long time ago. Things have changed since then."

"Yes, they have." She wiped her clammy hands on her denim skirt. "I am no longer that scared, insecure teenager."

"That's right." There was an odd note in his voice.

She knew what he was thinking. She was a grown, independent woman who made her own living and lived in a big beautiful house. A woman used to luxuries and conveniences she might not easily give up.

"I know what I want, Aidan, and it's up to me, not you, to decide where I belong." Her legs were trembling. "I belong with you, Aidan. We belong together."

His face worked, the control suddenly gone. He put his hands on her arms. "Please, Gwen, don't do this," he said hoarsely. "Don't make it harder than it is already."

"I don't understand," she said shakily. "I don't understand why you are doing this!" She fought to keep her voice calm. "Are you planning to come back?"

"I don't know what's going to happen. Not soon, anyway."

She went icy cold. "Tell me the truth, Aidan. Why can't I come with you?"

"Because it's not going to work!" he repeated, dropping his hands and turning back to the desk.

"Because of what I have become? Because I'm used to a comfortable life? Because I have a big house? Well, I don't care about any of it, Aidan! I don't care about the house!"

He tossed a stack of papers into the wastebasket and met her eyes. "Don't you?"

"No!" Impatiently, she wiped her hair out of her face. "Aidan, please, I want to be with you." She was begging. Oh, God, she could not stand this. Where was her maturity? Her self-respect?

A loud honking outside announced the taxi's arrival. He put his arms around her and kissed her, holding her tight. It was a hard kiss that had a frightening finality about it.

"Be happy, Gwen," he said, his voice unsteady. Another loud honking came from outside. He let go of her and picked up his luggage. Without another word, without looking back, he strode out of the house.

Gwen sat slumped at the table in Alice's kitchen. Her head seemed too heavy to hold up these days. It felt as if her body was sapped of strength.

"Gwen, you look like death warmed over," Alice said. "Aidan will come back." She poured a cup of coffee and put it in front of Gwen.

"He's not coming back. At least not to me." Even her voice sounded dead, like the rest of her felt—as if her spirit had disappeared along with all the joy and happiness in her life.

The lonely emptiness of the big house had screamed at her this evening and she'd got into the car and gone over to Alice's house. From the living room came faint sounds of laughter from some television sitcom Alice's husband was watching.

"Honey, he was in a hurry!" Alice said. "Think of the pressure he was under, the responsibility he has of having a whole hospital to run! Give him some time to get his thoughts in order."

It had been a week since Aidan had left and Gwen hadn't heard a word from him. She'd hardly slept, her mind trying frantically to analyze what had happened. Why had Aidan acted the way he had? Something was terribly wrong—had been wrong for days before he'd left, but she had no idea what it was. He could have said all manner of things, made other plans, even if he had not wanted her to come to Ecuador. He could have said he'd come back as soon as possible. That he loved her. That they'd figure out a way to make their relationship work, somehow.

There'd been no promises, no words of love. Nothing but a horrible, undeniable finality. After Aidan had left in the taxi, she had stood in the empty summer house while the anger, fear and despair raging inside her changed into numb shock.

She'd driven home on automatic pilot, and the days that had followed were blurred together in a swirling sea of misery.

I can't lose him again, came the voice inside her over and over. *I can't lose him again. He can't decide for me what I need and want.*

"You know," Alice went on, sitting down across from Gwen, "it takes more than two months to bridge the distance of twelve years. What had you expected? That there'd be instant perfection and instant harmony? That you'd get married immediately and live happily ever after just like that?"

Gwen glowered at her. "Yes!"

Alice laughed. "Well, it's nice to see you're so passionately romantic, but a little realism is necessary."

"Well, he dumped me. How's that for realism?"

Alice made a face. "I'm not going to cheer you up, am I?"

"No. I feel passionately miserable." Gwen leaned her chin on her hands and sighed heavily. "I'm beginning to dislike myself sincerely. I suppose that's a bad sign."

"It's a good sign. Maybe you'll do something about it."

Gwen grimaced and pushed herself to her feet. "I'll have to, because I'm beginning to get really bored with myself." She slung her purse over her shoulder and managed a smile. "Here I go, in search of a more positive frame of mind."

Which was easier said than done. With Churi gone and Aidan gone, her life seemed empty. Her house seemed empty. The next day, she walked aimlessly through the beautiful, empty rooms, as she had done every day since Aidan had left. Everything was so still, so quiet. This house needed the sounds of children, a family. She'd made a mistake deciding not to sell it.

She stood in the door to Churi's room. I can un-decide not to sell it, she thought. I can call the Realtor right now and tell her to put it on the market. She went down the stairs, feeling suddenly out of breath.

She reached for the phone and panic erupted inside her. Her heart began to pound louder and louder, hammering against her chest as if it wanted to jump right out. Her breathing was shallow and labored and perspiration streamed down her face and chest and back. The phone slipped out of damp hands and crashed onto the side table.

"Oh, God," she muttered, "not again."

She felt as if she were going to faint. Picking up the phone again, she dialed Alice's number, praying she would be home. She was.

"Alice," she gasped, "please help me. Please come."

"What's wrong?" Alice's voice was cool, com-posed—the nurse taking over instantly.

Gwen tried to swallow but couldn't. Her mouth was so dry she could barely talk. "I think ... I'm having...a panic attack. I'm going...to...faint."

"I'll be right there."

Slumped on the sofa, she waited for blackness to hit her, but it did not. Instead, she felt her heart begin to slow down. She tried to breathe as Aidan had told her the first time.

When she heard Alice's car drive up, she felt almost normal again.

"I'm here," Alice announced, walking into the living room.

"I think I'm all right now," Gwen said shakily, feeling relief wash over her. "I was so scared. My heart was going crazy and I couldn't breathe."

"You're drenched," Alice said matter-of-factly, sitting down next to her and picking up her wrist to feel her pulse. "Has this happened to you before?"

Gwen sucked in a deep breath. "Yes." She told Alice about the time she and Aidan had come home from seeing the rustic little house she'd decided to buy. "He said it might be because subconsciously I didn't want to give up the house."

Alice gave her a sharp look. "And what happened this time?"

Gwen swallowed with difficulty. "I was walking through the house and decided I had made a mistake deciding not to sell it. It makes no sense for me to keep this house when I'm all alone." She looked at her hand and saw it trembling. "I decided to change my mind, call the Realtor and tell her to put it on the market. I picked up the phone and then it happened."

Alice gave a faint smile. "I'm not a psychologist, but it seems to me that you don't really want to give up this house."

"I don't understand," Gwen said miserably. "Why not?"

"Marc had this house built for you."

"I know," Gwen said softly. "But Marc is dead, Alice, and we're never going to have the children we wanted."

"The mind is a strange piece of work," Alice said lightly, and Gwen couldn't help but smile.

"Maybe I'm going crazy."

"You're not going crazy. Your body is simply reacting to stress. Come to think of it, you're very lucky, because you're in a position to eliminate the stress. Just forget about selling the house. You probably just need more time."

"Time for what?"

"You probably think you've stopped grieving about Marc, but maybe you haven't."

Gwen shook her head slowly. Somewhere, on the fringes of her consciousness, a thought stirred, but she could not grasp the meaning of it and it disappeared.

Alice was wrong. She'd made her peace with the past and the circumstances of her marriage to Marc. After Alice had left, Gwen took a long, warm bubble bath and shampooed her hair, still damp from perspiration. Soaking in the tub was relaxing and she tried to empty her mind of disturbing thoughts.

That night she dreamed the same dream again—the dream of the children in the house, dancing and laughing. This time they all hugged her, one after the other, giving her damp, sticky kisses on her cheeks.

She awoke smiling, her arms clutching a pillow close to her chest.

She lay very quietly, not wanting to give up the joyful feeling of the dream. And suddenly, from her dream-filled mind, surfaced the realization why she did not want to sell the house.

It had nothing to do with the house itself. Or the fact that Marc had built it. The house had merely been a symbol for her vision—that joyous, hopeful dream vision of having a houseful of children to love and care for, the dream she had held in her mind ever since she was a lonely little girl.

It wasn't the house she didn't want to give up. It was the dream.

A light, exhilarating feeling filled her. Everything was clear, so clear. If she so deeply wanted children, she could have them. She could take in more foster children, she could adopt children. Nobody said you had to be married to have children.

From somewhere Aidan's face floated before her eyes, and a deep grief swept away her joy. "Aidan," she whispered, "oh, Aidan, I love you."

She'd left some things at Aidan's house and the next day she went over to pick them up. Ella would be there, she knew. She felt an unaccountable trepidation.

She found Ella in the kitchen, taking a can of Coke out of the fridge. She wore white denim shorts and a shirt of bright, sapphire-blue cotton and she was barefoot. Her toenails were painted a raspberry pink and she looked cool and fresh.

"I know you're working and I apologize for disturbing you," Gwen said, feeling ridiculously nervous. "But I was in the neighborhood and I thought I'd pick up some things I'd left here."

Ella smiled. "No problem. Come on in."

Gwen stepped into the kitchen, feeling a stranger, feeling awkward. She looked at Ella and Ella looked back. Ella's smile widened. "We were never introduced, I believe." She held out her hand. "I'm Ella Morton. I'm a colleague of Aidan's."

Alice smiled back. "I'm Gwen Silva. I thought you were Aidan's wife, at first."

Ella's brows shot up as she let out a laugh. "Nope, I'm taken already." She raised the Coke in her hand. "You want one?"

"I don't want to hold you up."

"I haven't seen a soul since I arrived here three days ago, except the housekeeper, and she's rather a morose type." Ella moved to the fridge and fished out another Coke. "Sit down."

They sat at the table facing each other, sipping the cold drink.

"Have you heard from Aidan?" Gwen asked casually, feeling the icy-cold can chilling her hand.

Ella shook her head. "Nope. It's hard getting through on the phone. And I imagine he's dealing with all kinds of problems and pulling long shifts and blanking out the rest of the universe while he concentrates." It sounded as if Ella had a pretty good idea of what was going on.

"How's the book coming?"

Ella frowned. "It would have worked better if Aidan had stayed here and I'd gone back." There was a note of impatience in her voice now. She shrugged. "I couldn't persuade him. He insisted on leaving."

He insisted on leaving. Gwen's hand trembled as she took in the meaning of the words: Aidan hadn't had to leave. Ella could have gone. It would have been better for finishing the book on time, better for the book that he valued so much.

Yet he had left, *wanted* to leave.

She felt sick. "Did he say why he thought he should go instead of you?" she heard herself ask.

Ella rolled her eyes. "He said since he was in charge of the project, it was his responsibility. He wanted nothing to go wrong. He came very close to seriously insulting my capabilities." Ella met Gwen's eyes, and one corner of her mouth curved in a half smile. "He has an overdeveloped sense of responsibility. Very annoying at times."

Gwen lifted the can and gulped more Coke, praying for composure. Putting the drink down, she pushed herself away from the table. "I'd better get going. Do you mind if I go and get my stuff?"

"No, no, of course not."

In a daze she went around and gathered up her things—a few clothes, a swimsuit, some toiletry articles, a book.

"Thanks for the Coke," she said as she was leaving. "Good luck with the book."

"Thanks." Hesitation flickered across Ella's face. "For what it's worth, as far as I know, Aidan isn't involved with anyone in Ecuador."

Gwen clutched her belongings hard against her chest as she stared at Ella's face. "Thanks," she said unsteadily. "I . . . I didn't think so." Actually, the thought had not even occurred to her. It wasn't in Aidan's nature to play that sort of game. Whatever his reason for leaving, it wasn't something like that.

He insisted on leaving. Ella's words kept haunting her all through the day and into the night. She lay sleeplessly in bed, contemplating the fact that Aidan had left when someone else could have gone just as well. Had it really been because of his overdeveloped sense of responsibility?

She didn't believe it for a minute.

Going back to Ecuador had been an opportunity to get away from her. She hugged her pillow to her chest, hard, trying not to feel the anguish.

"Oh, Aidan," she whispered into the dark. "Why?"

There had to be a reason why. Again, a whisper of awareness teased her mind. She wanted to grasp it, hold on to it, but it slipped away before she could transform it into conscious thought.

The open window revealed a dark patch of sky studded with stars. Insects chirped and shrieked, filling the air with sound. She gazed at the sky, praying for a miracle.

Two days later Gwen went over the calendar, counting the days for the third time. Her head felt oddly light. Her hand trembled. It wasn't possible. It *could* not be possible. The chances were one in thousands, according to statistics.

She counted again and again. There was no doubt.

She was pregnant.

CHAPTER NINE

"I'VE TRIED three different pregnancy testing kits,"
Gwen told the doctor. "They all came out positive.
Don't you dare tell me they were wrong."

The doctor laughed and perched on his examining stool. "Let's have a look at you first and ask
you some questions before I make my diagnosis."

Sometime later, his examination over, he confirmed the test kit results.

"You're pregnant, all right. Congratulations. Get
dressed and I'll see you in my office."

She had her clothes on in record time and sat
down on the other side of the doctor's desk. How
many times had she been here, sitting in this same
chair, filled with longing and hope?

"It's a miracle, you know," she said to the
doctor. "We were being perfectly responsible and
careful. I shouldn't be pregnant, but I am. It's a
miracle."

"Unless you were celibate, it's not a miracle,"
said the doctor dryly. "Certainly, from what you've
told me, the chances were extremely slim according
to statistics, but it wasn't impossible."

"I don't want to hear about statistics," she said,
looking at him loftily. "I prefer to think of it as
a miracle."

He inclined his gray head slightly, laughter in his blue eyes. "You have my permission. I consider all conceptions a miracle."

She glowered at him. "But mine is more special than others." *It's a sign, an omen*, she added silently.

He leaned back his head and laughed. "Of course."

Later, she walked out of the cool, white office into the bright summer sunshine. She lifted her head to the blue sky, feeling the breeze, the warmth of the sun and the joy was almost too much to bear. "Thank you, God," she whispered. She reached her arms to the sky, made a little leap and twirled around on the toes of one foot and laughed out loud.

Whistles broke into her consciousness. Coming to a stop, she faced three grinning workmen, leaning on their spades, apparently taking an entertainment break from digging a trench next to the building. Long hair, bare, suntanned chests, muddy, hip-hugging jeans.

"Hey, lady!" one of them called out. "Do that again!"

She laughed. "Next time!"

I'm going to have a baby. I'm going to have a baby of my very own. Her despair was gone. There was no room for anything but joy. No problem seemed insurmountable. Not even the problem of Aidan, the father of her baby, hiding from her on another continent. She no longer was a frightened eighteen-year-old. She could handle this. The question was how. All she needed to do was to apply her imagination and mind power and the solution would come to her.

And so it did, almost instantly. Her eyes caught the photo book on the coffee table. Her heart began to race with excitement. Of course!

She dialed Joe's number.

A week later they were on their way to Ecuador.

The market in the small town was a spectacle of color and sound. Women in pretty white-embroidered blouses and full skirts in vivid colors carefully selected fruits and vegetables for the evening meal. Their long black hair had been braided in two thick plaits and fedoras perched on the top of their heads—just like the pictures Gwen had seen. It all looked very festive, yet she felt as if she was not really in the middle of it, as if it were a daydream that wasn't real. Thoughts and images of Aidan dominated her mind and thoughts. All she could think of was what lay ahead when she would see him again this afternoon. How would he react when he saw her? What would he say?

It was important to stay positive, but it was not easy to quench the undercurrents of fear that ran through her head. In her mind she created a variety of scenarios, focusing only on the more encouraging possibilities.

Gwen bought some fruit and some *empanadas*, meat-filled wheat pastries, for lunch. "We'd better get back to the hotel," she said to Joe, who was totally entranced in photographing an old grandmother with her tiny baby granddaughter. "I don't want to miss that plane."

In a couple of hours she'd fly out to Aidan's highland town, an isolated place further north. It had taken her days, and a good dose of patience, to make the arrangements. She began to weave her way back through the stalls and the colorful throng of people. Joe followed her out regretfully. Ever since they'd arrived a few days ago, he'd been like a man possessed with his camera.

"Are you sure you don't want me to go with you?" Joe asked a while later. He was standing in the open door that separated their two hotel rooms, watching her pack a small bag. "I don't know if it's smart for you to be traveling alone in this place." He took a bite from one of the *empanadas*.

Gwen shook her head, glancing out the window of the small room, seeing a sweeping display of the tiled roofs against a dramatic backdrop of volcanic mountains rising into the crystalline blue sky.

"I'll be fine, Joe. This will give you a chance to work on your travel story in peace and I'll be back in a few days to work with the kids some more."

For several days they'd stayed in this small Spanish colonial town, talking to schoolchildren, taking photos. A Peace Corps volunteer was their guide and had introduced them to the school. Gwen loved the historic little town with its hilly streets, its cobbled plazas and balconied buildings. She loved the little school with its curious, brown-eyed children dressed in their colorful clothes.

She felt great. Only the faintest of nausea in the morning—just enough to remind her that she was really truly pregnant. Every time she thought of the baby, joy flooded her.

She thought of the baby now and grinned exuberantly at Joe. "I'll be fine, honest. I'm not going to get lost or anything. The plane will drop me off right where I need to be." She was glowing. She wanted to sing and dance, which was not such a good idea, being in a foreign country where they might think she'd gone over the edge. On the other hand, people liked singing and dancing here. Joe was watching her with amazement.

"What is up with you, Gwen? I can't remember ever seeing you this...exhilarated."

"It must be the thin air."

"Usually that has the opposite effect." He frowned unhappily. "I don't like the idea that Aidan doesn't know you're coming. I'm worried you might not find what you're expecting. Are you sure you're doing the right thing?"

"No," she said, "but I'm doing it anyway."

A few hours later that afternoon, a twin-engine turbo plane dropped her off at the small landing strip near the hospital in the arid mountain town. They'd flown over the Sierra, with its green, fertile valleys and volcanic peaks and Gwen had watched the scenery in awe—the green, cultivated hills, the cold, arid higher plateaus where nothing wanted to grow.

A Land Rover from the hospital was waiting at the airstrip to pick up medical supplies, and the driver was happy to give her a ride. The hospital was a low, whitewashed building with sky-blue window frames. As she climbed out of the Land

Rover, she heard the plane flying overhead, saw it disappearing from sight, and suddenly she felt quite alone and terrified. She sat down on a blue bench, trying to collect herself. She was here now, and the moment had arrived to face her destiny. She groaned at her own melodrama.

She glanced around. The one-storied building was a simple yet attractive place, the addition of colorful flower beds a cheerful note in the colorless surroundings of the town. It was larger than she had expected, then she remembered that it served a widespread area.

So this was the place where Aidan worked. He was here somewhere in this building, seeing patients, comforting children.

She hadn't seen him in a month.

She swallowed at the constriction in her throat, struggling with a fear she had not allowed entry in her consciousness earlier.

And then she saw him.

He came striding energetically along the path, white coat flapping, a stethoscope dangling from his pocket. His hair was a little too long. His face looked serious and preoccupied, his eyes staring off into the distance. This was Aidan, her man, the man she loved with all her heart and soul.

Her heart turned over. Warmth flooded her. She wanted to run and throw her arms around him, hold him, kiss him, feel his solid strength against her. She wanted to see a smile of surprise light up his face. He looked so sexy, so wonderful, she felt herself smiling just looking at him as he was coming toward her. Gwen held her breath, knowing that any moment now he would see her.

He stopped dead in his tracks and stared at her. "Gwen!" Something flashed in his eyes.

She jumped to her feet. "Aidan!" She grinned, unable to stop herself. "It's so good to see you."

She saw him swallow, saw his body grow rigid. Any hope she'd entertained of his face lighting up evaporated.

His face worked with dark emotions, then became an expressionless mask. "What the hell are you doing here?" he asked harshly.

"Working," she said promptly. "Joe and I are in the country to do another book." It was true enough.

He looked stunned for a moment. "You are what?"

"Doing another book. Joe's doing the photos, and I'm doing the interviews and drawings. I mean, the children are doing the drawings. They're adorable, Aidan! You should see what we already have! We've been here only for a few days, working in this little town and it's so exciting. What a great place!" She heard herself rambling on, could not curb the nervous energy and stop the words from flowing out. "It's an old Spanish colonial town with these fun houses with balconies hanging over the street, and the market is wonderful and—"

He shook her shoulders. "Be quiet!" he said roughly. "What the hell possessed you?"

She laughed. She couldn't help it. "What's wrong with my working in Ecuador? What's wrong with doing a book about Indian children?"

"What about your teaching job?"

"We found another teacher. Everything was arranged to everyone's satisfaction." She smiled. "It was amazing how well everything fell into place." The efficiency with which all the arrangements had been made only served to affirm in her that her decision to come to Ecuador had been the right one.

"Don't look so grim, Aidan. This is a wonderful opportunity." She widened her smile. "My horoscope told me that great and exciting things were awaiting me in a far and distant place. It didn't tell me which place, so I thought I might as well pick Ecuador. I want to talk to you about working with the children in the hospital—have them tell me their stories, and have them make drawings, if they're able to do that."

He glowered at her. "You think this is funny?"

"Funny? I don't know. I'm having the time of my life. I feel great. I'm happy. That's good, isn't it? Are you happy, Aidan?"

"What the hell is the matter with you?"

She gave him a wide-eyed look. "What do you mean?"

"Has someone introduced you to the joys of *chicha* already?" he asked coldly. He moved closer and looked into her eyes. "Are you drunk?"

She laughed. "Yes. I'm drunk with life. I'm high on life. I'm positively ecstatic."

"Are you taking drugs?"

"Vitamins," she said, biting her lip, trying to look solemn. It was too hard and she gave up and laughed.

He lowered her eyelid with a very clinical finger. She allowed the intrusion—she had nothing to hide.

She offered him her wrist. "Take my pulse, too, Doc."

He did not oblige. "Sky high, no doubt," he said grimly.

She nodded in agreement. "Of course it is. You're making it happen." She bit her lip again in another attempt not to laugh. She had no idea what was happening to her. A wild, impetuous force was taking over, making her throw all caution and inhibitions overboard.

His jaw tightened as he studied her face. "You should see yourself."

"I do! I'm looking at myself every chance I get. And I think I look pretty good." She grinned. "Radiant, actually. I look radiant. Don't you think?"

He raised his eyes heavenward as if pleading for divine assistance. "I have no time for this. For God's sake, you can't be here, Gwen!"

She crossed her arms in front of her chest. "In case it had escaped your attention, I already am here." She looked straight into his eyes.

"You're going back." His voice was hard, his face angry.

She did not waver, did not avert her eyes. "No, I'm not. I have a job to do and I'm not leaving until I decide so myself." She smiled with determination. "I'm a very independent person, and I make my own decisions."

"Admirable," he said cooly, "but it is my decision whether you'll stay here or not. And you're not."

Her stomach churned with sudden anxiety. She willed herself not to give in to it. "We have to talk."

He shoved his hands in the pockets of his lab coat. "No, and you can't stay here."

"Not even tonight?" she asked, wide-eyed, feigning lightness. "You're going to throw me out in the hostile, dark, Andean night?" *Me, a pregnant woman*? she almost added.

His face was an impenetrable mask. "For tonight I suppose there's no choice. You'll have to stay at my house. But tomorrow morning I'll put you on the bus myself, to wherever you want to go."

CHAPTER TEN

"COME along." Aidan picked up her bag and began to stride off. For a moment Gwen just stood there, watching his back moving away from her. All lightness and humor had disappeared. With an effort she forced down the fear.

"Aidan, wait!"

He stopped, turning slowly. His whole body was tensed. "Going too fast for you?"

"Yes." She swallowed, her heart racing, and looked into his eyes. "Am I really so terribly unwelcome?"

For a moment he said nothing, and she wondered if she saw the struggle in his eyes. A muscle moved near his mouth. She felt a twinge of hope. Maybe he wasn't quite as immune as he tried to appear.

"I wasn't expecting you," he said noncommittally. "We're not well-organized for visitors of the healthy variety."

Visitor. She swallowed hard. It did not sound promising. "I'm not a very demanding visitor," she said lightly. *All I want is your love and your eternal devotion*, she elaborated silently.

"That's just as well, because if you were you'd be severely tested."

"I'm already being severely tested," she shot back, "and it's not because of any lack in creature comforts."

He turned without answering and resumed walking. Picking up the bag of fruit she had bought at the market that morning, she followed him, having no other choice. *Damn you, Aidan*, she said to his broad back. What is the matter with you?

He led her to a small bungalow on the hospital compound. It was simple, but comfortable enough. One wall of the living room was given to bookshelves that reached to the ceiling and every inch of them was crammed full of books and magazines. No sign of a TV, but there was a small stereo system on a low cabinet and an impressive collection of music tapes.

He introduced her to a tiny, wrinkled Indian woman, who kept house for him. Maria had piercing black eyes, and the traditional long braids, and she wore a voluminous, bright blue skirt.

Gwen handed her the fruit. "I brought some fruit at the market this morning," she said to Aidan in explanation. "I remember you saying it's hard to get here."

"Thank you," he said politely. "Let me show you your room." It was small, furnished with a simple cot, not made up, a straight chair, a dresser and a small bedside table. The window offered a dramatic view of stark mountains against a cool blue sky.

Aidan put her bag on the bed. "The bathroom is straight across the corridor. If you need anything, ask Maria. She'll be right here to make the bed.''

"Thank you," she said again, feeling her spirits crash even further at his polite and businesslike tone. Nothing was left of her earlier elation. He didn't want her here. It was humiliating.

He crossed his arms in front of his chest and perused her face with cool gray eyes. "For your own good, Gwen, don't get any ideas about staying here. It's not going to work."

"Is there somebody else?" The question came out without her having thought about it.

A muscle jerked on the left side of his face. "It's irrelevant whether there is or not. Now, if you'll excuse me, I have to get back to the hospital. I'll be home for dinner around seven."

She stood alone in the room, hands clenched by her side, feeling like an unwanted package. Some welcome this was! But there was no turning back now. She was good and stuck in this desolate town, at least until tomorrow.

Why was she doing this to herself? What had she expected? Somewhere deep inside she had hoped for a fairy tale, for Aidan crushing her to him, saying he'd almost died of loneliness, saying he was never going to let her go again, saying he would love her for the rest of his life. What she'd hoped for was a prince, but what she was getting was an imperfect human being whose reasons and motivations she didn't understand. A man who might not love her at all anymore.

The walls of the small house seemed to close in on her. It was hard to breathe, which was no mystery considering the high altitude.

She fled out of the house, not knowing what to do, just knowing she had to get out. She began to walk, across the hospital compound, out the main gates, down the dusty road into the small town. Many of the houses were made of mud bricks and wood with thatched roofs. She watched the women in their colorful garb peeling potatoes and working on primitive weaving looms outside the simple buildings. Others were cooking food on a spit over an open fire. Guinea pigs, she knew, and tried not to dwell in it. Children looked at her curiously, their dark eyes wide and innocent. Chickens pecked through the barren dirt, searching for food. A scrawny dog followed her for a while, then disappeared. The sights did nothing to lift her spirits, and she turned back to the house.

Maria had made the bed, and she lay down on it and stared at the patch of cool blue sky visible from the small window. Not a cloud in sight. A beautiful sky—clean and bright.

She took in deep breaths and tried to relax her body. Everything felt tight and tense. Beginning with her toes and working upward, she relaxed her muscles, one at a time, trying to work out the tension. Marc, years ago, had taught her how to do it.

Marc. She could think of him now without guilt, without pain. It was good. It was right.

She wasn't sure how long she lay there, her body heavy now, looking at the cool blue sky, feeling a little drowsy, when suddenly Alice's words floated through her thoughts. *You probably think you've stopped grieving over Marc, but you haven't.* Another thought tagged along, right behind. *Aidan might have thought the same thing. Might still think the same thing.*

She jerked upright in the bed, her heart racing. Oh, God, she thought. That's it! That's why!

Everything fit—like a puzzle. Memories rushed into her mind—words Aidan had said, the way he had behaved, the expressions in his eyes she had not understood. All of it fit a pattern.

She lay back down and groaned as she closed her eyes. How could she have been so deaf and blind? How could she not have known?

Aidan came back a little after seven. Gwen was sitting in one of the simple wooden chairs, trying not to appear too nervous. It was not easy. He closed the door behind him and gave her only a passing glance.

"I'll wash up and we'll eat," he informed her.

Dinner was a simple, rather bland stew with potatoes and vegetables, cooked and served by Maria. Some of the fruit she had brought lay on a plate, ready to eat. She didn't even know what some of them were—exotic fruit she had never seen before.

Aidan ate in silence and she knew it was better now than later to start a conversation that was not going to be easy. She wanted to get it over with.

"After you left, a couple of weeks ago," she began, "I went to pick up some things I had left at your house. I talked to Ella."

"Yes?" He glanced up politely.

"She told me she'd offered to go back to Ecuador but that you insisted on going."

"So I did." His tone gave nothing away.

"I want you to tell me why you left me the way you did. You owe me the truth—you owe me that much."

"I saw no good reason to continue our relationship." The words were cool, businesslike, and razor sharp. She felt herself wince. She gathered courage, knowing there was only one way to deal with him, to break through the wall.

"You were jealous of Marc," she said, delivering the statement in an equally cool and businesslike manner. "I understand that now."

He cocked an arrogant brow. "Marc is dead," he said succinctly.

"So he is." Her gaze did not waver, challenging him, searching his face, probing beneath the cool mask. The silence vibrated with tension.

A muscle worked in his left cheek. "You weren't ready to let go," he said finally. "You couldn't even bring yourself to sell his goddamned house!"

Her heart contracted. "It wasn't because I couldn't let go of Marc, Aidan," she said softly. "It wasn't that at all."

He looked at her stonily. "That's certainly the way it looked to me."

"And that's why you left? Because you thought I wasn't over Marc?" She swallowed. "You were jealous. Jealous because he showed me the world, jealous because I loved him, jealous because I couldn't give up the house, or *thought* I could not."

"Thanks for the analysis," he said with chilling sarcasm. "The way I see it is that you weren't letting go. You wouldn't hear the truth about him and his selfishness! You seemed to think of him as some sort of superior being. You went into a panic attack just *thinking* about selling the house. Forgive me if that didn't give me a lot of confidence in the viability of our relationship." He jabbed his fork into a piece of potato. "Now, may we change the subject?"

She clenched her hands in her lap. She was trembling so hard, it was difficult to speak. "No. I'm not finished. I had some emotional trouble selling the house, but it had nothing to do with Marc."

"Oh, really?" His scornful tone spoke volumes.

"Yes, really. I didn't understand why I felt the way I did until later. The house was only a symbol for...for the dream I've had ever since I was little."

He said nothing, leaning back in his chair, giving her a skeptical look.

"You know I always wanted children," she went on. "Well, if I'd bought the little house we looked at together, I could never have these children. They wouldn't fit, you see. I couldn't live there and keep that vision alive. And subconsciously I couldn't let go of that vision—it was too much a part of me and I just couldn't abandon it, no matter how unrealistic it might seem at the time. That's why I had that panic attack." She took in a deep breath. "The house was a symbol of that vision."

"And a symbol of your marriage," he added coldly.

"Aidan, Marc is dead! He was an important part of my life, a *necessary* part of my life, but it's over and I've come to terms with the realities of our relationship."

"You loved him," he said harshly.

Her heart lurched. "Yes, I did. There are all kinds of love, Aidan."

"And what kind was that?"

"We were friends. We liked and respected each other." She swallowed. "We were both hurting and we needed each other."

He stared at her, silent, waiting, the knowledge dawning in his eyes. And something else—a guardedness.

"I told you I felt guilty for not loving him better," she said with difficulty. "I felt guilty because I knew how it could be, and it wasn't like that. I know how it could be because I loved you. What you and I had was special and it never was like that with Marc. It'll never be like that with anyone else. What we have between us...it goes beyond friendship, beyond respect...it's the real thing."

"From what I understand, what you had with Marc was pretty real." His face was hard.

Despair flooded her, mixed with anger. "I don't know what it takes to convince you! Maybe you never felt what I felt. Maybe it was just an illusion on my part. Maybe you never felt anything special for me this summer. Maybe all it was was just a run-of-the-mill summer fling! Dumb, naive me to think we could still love each other after all these years—that we could make it work this time." She scraped her chair back, only one thing on her mind—to get away from him.

A loud knocking came on the door, which flew open almost immediately. A young nurse stood in the door, almost tripping over her own words as she said something about an accident and blood and hurry. Before Gwen had digested what was going on, Aidan had leapt to his feet and was gone out the door.

Alone in the silent house, Gwen felt the despair crawl through her. A deep exhaustion settled over her, as if she'd scaled a mountain and all her strength had been used up.

Even taking a shower was a struggle. Finished, she climbed into the narrow bed hoping for the oblivion of sleep. It wouldn't be good to let herself get too run down; she needed her rest.

But sleep did not claim her; her mind churned with uneasy thoughts. What if she couldn't convince Aidan? What if he had no confidence in their love? What if he did not want her anymore? She'd still have to tell him about the baby. She rested her hand on her abdomen. He had the right to know.

Shades of the past. Images of her mother as a young girl, alone in a shabby motel room, pregnant, with ten dollars to her name. *No*! she told herself. *This is different*!

She was not alone—she had friends at home who loved her and would give her support. She had considerably more than ten dollars to her name. She was not a young girl. She was an independent woman with a life of her own, a house, a job. Having a child would be a joy, not a burden.

She rested her hand on her abdomen. No outward sign yet of a baby, but it was there, safe inside her, growing every day.

But she didn't want to have it alone, raise it alone. She wanted Aidan with her. She shivered, realizing she was cold. The window was open and the night air on this high mountain plateau was chilly. She stumbled to her feet and closed the window, huddling back under the blankets.

Aidan might not want her, but he most certainly would want his own baby. Not in a thousand years would he send her off with a ten-dollar bill in her hand. The image was so preposterous, she found herself laughing.

Of course, Aidan could tell her he thought the baby wasn't his. It was Joe's, or somebody else's. For a moment she contemplated that scenario, then tossed it out. Aidan wouldn't make it as the scumbucket of the year if he tried.

Everything is going to work out right, she told herself fiercely.

It had to. She could not afford to think otherwise. Don't think, she told herself. Don't think. Tomorrow is another day. Tomorrow there will be plenty of time for thinking.

She dreamed of the children in the school she and Joe had visited. She dreamed of Aidan. Aidan smiling, touching her face, stroking her hair.

It was all a mistake. He loved her. He wouldn't let her go again. Warmth surrounded her and she was no longer cold.

His hands again, on her body, stroking. It felt so good, so good. His face against hers, his mouth caressing her eyelids, her temples, his whole body against hers, so hot and deliciously exciting.

She sighed and stirred, turning slightly. She heard a sound from outside, a bird, something. She moaned, keeping her eyes tightly closed. She did not want to wake up. She wanted to hold on to the dream, to the warmth.

"Aidan," she whispered, "I love you."

"I love you, too."

She smiled, sighing again, and then she felt his mouth on hers, his kiss . . . real, so very real.

She wasn't dreaming.

Her hand was touching warm skin. Warm, alive, real skin. No dream, this. No figment of her imagination.

"Aidan?" she whispered, breathless.

"Yes?"

"I thought I was dreaming," she said softly, afraid to break the spell.

"What were you dreaming?"

"That you're making love to me. I was afraid to wake up." She put her arms around him and held on to him so tight that he gave a soft groan of protest. She relaxed her arms. "Oh, Aidan, I can't believe it. Are you really here?"

"I'm really here." His mouth covered hers before she could say anything. He kissed her with a fierce but loving passion, and all thought left her head. All she could do was revel in the wonderful feeling of joy and excitement, the delicious hunger stirring in her body, tingling through her blood. No doubt in her mind, no worry, no fear.

They made magic together—their own special magic that belonged only to them.

"Tell me what you thought when you saw me yesterday," Gwen whispered as the golden dawn crept through the window.

Aidan threw one brown arm across his eyes and groaned. "I panicked."

"You didn't look panicked to me. You looked furious."

He grimaced. "It's amazing what we do to disguise our true feelings."

"Why did you panic when you saw me?"

"I was afraid I could not resist you."

"Well, you didn't." She chuckled. "Was it so terrible? I thought it was rather wonderful, actually." She played idly with his chest hair. He grabbed her hand.

"Yes, it was."

"What made you give in? What changed your mind?"

He closed his eyes and a fleeting expression of pain flashed across his features. "The nurse came to get me after dinner last night because they'd brought in a busload of people injured in a crash. I stood there in the operating room patching up little kids' injuries and all I could think of was that life is too short for anger and wounded pride and all the rest. Deep inside I knew very well that I was rejecting a chance of happiness with you because of misguided male pride and unfounded jealousy. I just needed a good shock to admit to it."

"It must have been awful," she said softly. "I'm sorry."

"Let's not dwell on it," he said. "I just want to hold you and kiss you and make love to you again." He kissed her tenderly. "Tell me it's true what you said last night," he added huskily.

"What?"

"That what we had...have is special."

Her heart turned over. "It is. You know it is. What I feel for you I can never feel for anybody else. It belongs to us, Aidan. It always did."

"I was a jealous bastard," he said thickly. "I'm sorry for hurting you."

"I hurt you, too." She buried her face in the warm hollow of his neck. "Oh, Aidan, I want so much to start over, to make a new beginning, to be happy."

"Yes." He stroked her hair. "I missed you terribly. I was so miserable after I left you."

"Me, too," she whispered, and a little devil stirred inside her. "For a little while, anyway," she added lightly.

A slight pause. "A little while?"

"Yeah, I decided to give it up."

"Give it up?"

She looked into his eyes and grinned. "A miracle happened."

He rolled his eyes, and she laughed. "A divine sign, an omen, something indescribably beautiful."

He dragged the pillow over his head and moaned. "I don't believe in miracles."

"You'll have to."

"Try me."

She pulled the pillow away from his face and smiled into his eyes. It felt like all of her was smiling, a soft warm glow radiating from her, toward him, enveloping him. "I'm pregnant. We're going to have a baby."

He looked at her in stunned silence, then shook his head. "Gwen, I . . . you must be mistaken."

His disbelief did not surprise her and she kept her smile in place. "I'm not mistaken."

"I . . . we . . . we didn't take any chances, ever. It's just not . . ." He rubbed his chin. "Statistically, I suppose it's possible, but—" He was stumbling over his words and she laughed as she put her hand over his mouth for an instant.

"Don't talk statistics," she said softly. "It's a miracle. An affirmation."

His face worked. "Gwen, are you absolutely sure?"

She nodded. "Confirmed by three drugstore test kits and one gray-haired gynecologist-obstetrician with a lifetime of experience."

With a smothered groan he put his arms around her and pulled her down onto his chest. "Oh, Gwen, I love you," he said thickly. "I love you with all my heart and all my soul."

Her heart flowed over. "I love you, too—with all my heart and all my soul."

They lay silently in each other's arms, savoring the words, and the depth of their feelings—mystic music dancing in their hearts.

Finally, he stirred. "*Three* test kits?" he asked softly, humor in his voice now.

She chuckled, her mouth stroking his hair-roughened chest. "Yes."

"Why didn't you tell me right away?" he asked.

"I wanted things to be right between us first. I wanted you to know I always loved you, that..." She paused and took in a deep breath. "That Marc and my memories of him are no threat to you, or us." She tightened her arms around him. "I knew you'd never deny your responsibility for the baby, but I...I didn't want you to want me because of that." Her voice was shaky. "I wanted to know...that you wanted me...for me."

He hugged her convulsively. "My stupid pride could have cost me your love and the baby, as well."

"I would have told you about the baby no matter what you decided about me, but I really wanted it to be a special moment when I told you."

He kissed her fiercely. "I love you," he said huskily. "I always did, I always will. I'm not going to let you out of my sight again until we're married."

Her heart leapt. "And I'm not letting you out of my sight, either. So we should be safe."

He moved her a little and sat up, pulling her up with him, close in the narrow bed. "We'll have to figure out a plan."

"I'm going to stay here with you."

He frowned. "It won't be easy."

"I'm tough."

He nodded. "True. My part of the project has another year to run, then I'm free."

"We can go somewhere else exotic," she suggested.

"Or we can go home and I can lecture and write."

"You'd rather be practicing medicine," she said, "and there's no way I'm going to ask you not to, besides there are vast parts of the world I haven't seen yet, and I want to. You can show me."

He gave her a crooked smile, his eyes full of love. "You are some fantastic woman," he said.

She smiled back at him, feeling his words fill her heart. "Of course, I'm having your baby."

"You're having my baby," he repeated slowly, trying out the words. "My baby. Our baby. Yours and mine."

Her throat closed with emotion. "Yes," she said huskily. "Think about it, Aidan. The baby is ours, just ours. It has nothing to do with the past, nothing at all. The baby is the future."

He heaved a great sigh, as if a terrible burden had been lifted from his shoulders. "When is it due?"

"April twelfth."

"How are you feeling?"

"High on life. Drugged on vitamins. Radiant, glorious and supremely healthy," she said promptly.

He moaned. "I deserved that, I suppose."

"Did you really think I was doing something stupid or illegal?"

"I couldn't imagine what was the matter with you."

She chuckled. "And you, a doctor. You should have seen it was a case of rampant female hormones doing their thing."

"So I'm not perfect."

"No, but you're very, very good," she said meaningfully. She took his hand and put it on her belly and smiled into his eyes. "You're a miracle maker."

MILLS & BOON

Affairs to REMEMBER

Stories of love you'll treasure forever...

Popular Australian author Miranda Lee brings you a brand new trilogy within the Romance line–
Affairs to Remember.

Based around a special affair of a lifetime, each book is packed full of sensuality with some unusual features and twists along the way!

This is Miranda Lee at her very best.

Look out for:

A Kiss To Remember in February '96

A Weekend To Remember in March '96

A Woman To Remember in April '96

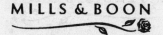

MILLS & BOON

Don't miss our great new series within the Romance line…

Landon's Legacy

One book a month focusing on each of the four members of the Landon family—three brothers and one sister—and the effect the death of their father has on their lives.

You won't want to miss any of these involving, passionate stories all written by Sandra Marton.

Look out for:

An Indecent Proposal in January '96
Guardian Groom in February '96
Hollywood Wedding in March '96
Spring Bride in April '96

Cade, Grant, Zach and Kyra Landon—four people who find love and marriage as a result of their legacy.

MILLS & BOON

Today's Woman

Mills & Boon brings you a new series of seven
fantastic romances by some of your favourite
authors. One for every day of the week in fact
and each featuring a truly wonderful woman
who's story fits the lines of the old rhyme
'Monday's child is...'

Look out for Eva Rutland's *Private Dancer*
in January '96.

Tuesday's child Terri Thompson is certainly full
of grace but will that be enough to win the love
of journalist Mark Denton—a man intent on
thinking the worst of her?

GET 4 BOOKS
AND A MYSTERY GIFT

Return this coupon and we'll send you 4 Mills & Boon Romances and a mystery gift absolutely FREE! We'll even pay the postage and packing for you.

We're making you this offer to introduce you to the benefits of Reader Service: FREE home delivery of brand-new Mills & Boon romances, at least a month before they are available in the shops, FREE gifts and a monthly Newsletter packed with information.

Accepting these FREE books and gift places you under no obligation to buy, you may cancel at any time, even after receiving just your free shipment. Simply complete the coupon below and send it to:

MILLS & BOON READER SERVICE, FREEPOST, CROYDON, SURREY, CR9 3WZ.

No stamp needed

Yes, please send me 4 free Mills & Boon Romances and a mystery gift. I understand that unless you hear from me, I will receive 6 superb new titles every month for just £1.99* each postage and packing free. I am under no obligation to purchase any books and I may cancel or suspend my subscription at any time, but the free books and gifts will be mine to keep in any case. (I am over 18 years of age)

1EP6R

Ms/Mrs/Miss/Mr _____

Address _____

_____

_____ Postcode _____

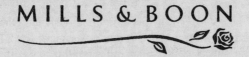

MILLS & BOON

Next Month's Romances

Each month you can choose from a wide variety of romance with Mills & Boon. Below are the new titles to look out for next month.

ANGRY DESIRE	Charlotte Lamb
THE VALENTINE CHILD	Jacqueline Baird
THE UNFAITHFUL WIFE	Lynne Graham
A KISS TO REMEMBER	Miranda Lee
GUARDIAN GROOM	Sandra Marton
PRIVATE DANCER	Eva Rutland
THE MARRIAGE SOLUTION	Helen Brooks
SECOND HONEYMOON	Sandra Field
MARRIAGE VOWS	Rosalie Ash
THE WEDDING DECEPTION	Kay Thorpe
THE HERO TRAP	Rosemary Badger
FORSAKING ALL OTHERS	Susanne McCarthy
RELENTLESS SEDUCTION	Kim Lawrence
PILLOW TALK	Rebecca King
EVERY WOMAN'S DREAM	Bethany Campbell
A BRIDE FOR RANSOM	Renee Roszel